Do Not Wake The Beast

Patricia I. Williams

MYTHICAL LEGENDS PUBLISHING

Do Not Wake the Beast is a work of fiction. The characters, incidents, and dialogs are products of the author's imagination and are not to be construed as real. Any resemblance to actual events or persons, living or dead, is entirely coincidental.

A Mythical Legends Publishing
Paperback Edition

Copyright © 2016 by Patricia I. Williams
Published by Mythical Legends Publishers, 2017
Publisher@mythicallegends.com
http://mythicallegends.com

ISBN-10: **1-943958-93-9**
ISBN-13: **978-1-943958-93-1**

Printed in America
9 8 7 6 5 4 3 2

To Our Heavenly Father. He never loses faith that we will rise above the temporal world no matter how far we fall.

Robert E. Howard because his stories expressed the love of right, even when the heroes acted unaware of their hand in it.

To J Carrell Jones, always inspiring, always pursuing knowledge, always a friend.

To Our Heavenly Father. He never loses faith that we will rise above the temporal world no matter how far we fall.

Robert E. Howard because his stories expressed the love of right, even when the heroes acted unaware of their hand in it.

To J Carrell Jones, always inspiring, always pursuing knowledge, always a friend.

Do Not Wake The Beast

Patricia I. Williams

DO NOT WAKE THE BEAST

The tavern door opened, then smacked against the wall so hard the timbers shivered and creaked. The startled inhabitants could only gap as the storm rushed in chilling their already wet bodies. Sleet and icy rain swirled through doorway and spat upon the patrons relegated to the dirt floor near it. Some grumbled and scuttled away from the muddy puddles as ice and rain pelted the interior. The barkeep rushed to close the door only to shriek when a dark shadow detached itself from the storm, moving into the common room.

The shaggy apparition moved the frightened man aside by stepping into his space. The door swung back and closed with another bang. The bar dropped across it, leaving the bitter weather to slap and push from the outside. A rough cloak dropped from a set of massive shoulders. The collective sighed with relief at the tall male figure. Oh, well not a demon, just another mercenary.

Raven hung his dripping cloak on the hook near

the door and rung the water from the dark braid draped around his neck. He already knew how many men sat at the greasy tables and that any women here had long since gone to bed in the cramped musty upper rooms. He turned on the still stupefied bartender.

"Boil some water, now."

"Water, boil water?"

"Water, now."

Raven crossed the dark room, removing the sword hanging from his back to a table nearest the soot darkened back wall. He pulled the table away and settled in the rickety chair that groaned under his weight. He ignored the bleary eyes peering at him and the stench of wet unwashed bodies. He took a leather pouch from the thick belt he wore and placed it on the table along with his damp travel bag. The barkeep rushed to the table holding a battered kettle, the handle wrapped by the bottom of his dirty apron.

"A tankard and the kettle before the water's cold." Raven growled at the seemingly witless man.

"Oh, yes, a tankard. Yes...yes sir...I yes." He scurried away again the kettle swinging wildly, causing swearing occupants of the floor and tables to duck and move from his path. Raven glared. The man finally stumbled back, dropping the tankard so it rolled across the table. The warrior's hand closed around it. The kettle banged against the side of the table, splashing water on the hapless bartender. He managed to put the kettle down and back away. One more glance from the warrior at the table sent him back to his duties on trembling legs.

Raven poured a portion of dried herbs into the tankard and filled it with water. He warmed his cold hands in the steam from the cup. After a few minutes he raised it to his lips. The first sip nearly forced a groan from the exhausted man. He had to really control the urge to gulp the bitter liquid down and scald his throat. The heat settled in his belly, warming him completely after a while. He finally relaxed against the wall and let his eyes travel openly around the room. Most of the inhabitants avoided his gaze.

There were just as many brigands as honest travelers in the room. His size and the gleaming steel of his sword should prevent any one from getting ideas about lifting his purse. He chuckled out loud at the thought because his purse was painfully thin right now. He was hoarding what remained in anticipation of a new job, hence the smelly hovel having to do for for this moment. He rested his head on the wall to doze, at least content the tavern was shielded by a hill that blocked the winds from blowing through the ill fitted logs at his back. He did not move as the people in the room finally settled once more before the meager fire.

The strong slept near the flames, the not so bold lay

shivering in the cold and enduring the draft whistling through the ramshackle walls and around the ill fitted door. After a while, Raven pulled a woolen blanket from his pack and wrapped it around himself. He allowed himself to relax, just a little, in the heavy folds and went to sleep.

Silence awakened him. The storm was over for now. He folded the blanket tightly and stuffed it into his pack. He knew the sun had risen, although he expected the day would be sullen with clouds, fog and more rain. The slide of metal on leather stirred some of the other wayfarers. Grabbing his still damp cloak, Raven stepped across bodies on the floor and lifted the bar from the door. He slipped into the chilly morning, crossing quickly to the shed to fetch his horses. The animals were nosing around in ice-rimmed hay. He slipped a bag of oats over their noses and rubbed them down before tossing blanket and saddle on his mount. Very soon, the animal would refuse the grains and need to hunt or Raven would have to buy fresh meat. He reloaded all his gear on the shaggy packhorse and stepped into the saddle.

Chi walked carefully, wary of the cracking ice and mud sliding beneath his hooves. Raven looked around at the dull winter landscape and figured he had at least a six-hour ride to the next tavern along the twisting, treacherous track passing for a road. He hoped to make it before the weather soured again. Another night in a filthy roadside tavern would not improve his mood. Sighing heavily, he guided his animals off into the tall pines, growling as wind blown water cascaded down from the trees. The rumble of distant thunder herald another round of storms.

The mercenary had heard a local lord, new to his position, was hiring men-at-arms to shore up his troops. Fighters from all over the Midlands were finding their way to these sparsely populated mountains. NorBlad raiders would be scouring the land very soon. It was said the old master of the lands paid tribute to the northern fighters but the peasants and lesser nobles still lost too much to the raiders. There should be fighting aplenty and gold for his war bag.

From time to time he dozed in the saddle aware that Chi would let him know if trouble approached.

Like him, the animal stood out in this land of dark pine forest and snow. Iron gray with black stockings, mane and tail, his muzzle and face were black as well. Chi hailed from the far western plains. The animal enabled the mercenary to charge twice the fees offered for only his sword. More than once Raven had literally been plucked from death's jaws by his oft times vicious guardian. Chi was heavily boned and muscled with deceptively gentle dark eyes. His teeth were dagger long and sharp edged, dealing deep and grievous wounds.

Tales were told that they were not true horses, but demon spawn erupting on the western plains during a fight between the gods. Raven always wondered if there was more truth than not to the tale. The demons chose their riders and seemed to anticipate their needs. They also had a sack of gall in their throats, which injected into a bite caused a lingering agonizing death. No one else rode him, no one dared. Savage, the animals were known to kill other four legs for food including their own kind.

*****

Torches were just being lit within the timber walled city of Virgilia when Raven finally reached the gate days later. The guardsmen paid little attention to Chi. In the dark he appeared just like any other horse and Raven was grateful. He had no wish to spend the evening in the cold arguing with superstitious men. Once inside he realized the city was teeming with people.

Observation determined many of the farmers from the countryside had moved into the city. Resigned to a longer wait for bed and a meal, Raven traveled through the town until arriving on the paths just below the high road to the lord's residence. Taverns, choked with smoke and rank odors, rang with off key music and fighting. The upper paths hosted the higher priced inns for the more sedate clientele. There would be people from the richer farms, merchants and nobles. Raven listened to the chatter from the throng pushing and shoving along the narrow torch lit way. Though disconcerted at finding a horse barring their way, most of the people were too inebriated to do more than stumble from his path. Hawkers stood in front of the doors, shouting about the best wines, feather mattresses and of course who had the fattest and cleanest bed warmers. He pondered over the gold left in his purse and finally decided to move a little closer to his goal. The best place would have a large barn where Chi could rest away from the majority of animals. Oddly, though he was a stallion, the animal did not insight other horses to fight, but they were very nervous around him.

He came to a place with a gate and a wall nearly his height surrounding it. Lamps and a bell hung from the posts. Further along the wall he could see an even wider gate, probably for carriages and wagons to come and go. Faint music could be heard over the rabble in the road. Decision made, he rang the bell.

After a time, a small head popped up under the bell.

"An ya bizna bein'?"

"What else would I be here for? Open the gate brat!"

"Tha li ya havin' na coin!" The guardian of the gate assessed Raven with an exaggerated leer only to have a hand surround his head and lift him from his perch.

"Open the damn gate, or I will open it with your head." Raven growled, squeezing the bug-eyed boy's skull. Torchlight reflected in the catlike eyes of the monster crushing his head. Frightened spitless, the youngster scrabbled at the wooden bar, arms and legs flailing wildly. He managed to lift it just enough that Raven dropped him and grabbed the heavy log. It was little effort to toss the bar over the head of the boy. He flinched as it hit the ground, one end narrowly missing his head. Chi pushed through the gate and the boy scrambled from his path.

"You don't decide for a man where his coin is spent brat. Keepers of gates can be slaves on the morrow."

The gulp was audible as the boy scrambled to his feet and hurried to get the bar back up on the gate. He would endure the dampness of his ragged britches for the remainder of his shift, but have two fights later on unable to endure the taunting about his smelly condition.

Raven rode across the yard and stepped down before the main doors of a very large inn. To one side he could see a taproom filled with revelers. Well to do nobles and merchants communed together. Tomorrow in his lordships residence they would pretend ignorance of each other. He stepped through double doors. The main lobby was well lit and he was not surprised to see a very fat tavern keeper leaning against a podium.

This one obviously trusted no one to collect his coin. How else could he maintain the mountain of flesh that covered his slim bones? Raven stepped up to the counter. Before the man could launch into his tirade the mercenary dropped a very small bag on the ledger book.

"See here now..."

"Look in the pouch before you give me any sass, old man."

Insulted, the man just prevented himself from calling for his bouncers. He untied the drawstring and poured two gold coins into this palm. Instantly his expression changed, to suspicion.

"I'm no thief, you greedy bastard. Say I am and taste steel."

"I, I would not dream of it. No sir, did...did not, er... cross my mind."

Raven scowled at the innkeeper. The man visibly shrank under the pale silver gaze of the mercenary.

"How many nights will that buy me and care for my horses?"

The coins disappeared into the chubby hands, then the man sank his teeth into the coin. On further inspection a smile creased his face until his eyes disappeared. His bite left marks in the soft metal.

"Forgive me sir, a man cannot be too careful in these trying times. Come, come this way. Why I will escort you myself. Yes yes, this will afford you one of our best rooms and food for at least a moon."

"My animals need tending and my bags brought in."

"I have ser..."

"I tend my own things."

"As you wish...of course. Right this way."

Raven followed the man up two flights of stairs and a turn to the left. The room was larger than expected and the bed even larger. Servants scurried in behind him, rushing to light the kindling in the fireplace and turn back the covers. The innkeeper lit the candles in the scones near the door. A pitcher of water and a basin were brought in. He checked the bed, pleasantly surprised to find it feathered and not filled with straw. The covers were soft wool and it even had pillows. There were no connecting doors and the one window looked out over the rear yard. That pleased him. The barn was directly across from his room.

"This will do innkeeper. Bring whatever you have left in your kitchen this hour for a hungry man. I do not expect a full meal this late. Listen closely to what I tell you. I do not require wine or ale. A good strong tea is all right, if you have it. If not, keep hot water on boil for me. I have my own herbs and I drink at odd times. I like my food cooked plain. Leave the fancy sauces for those in your taproom. A tub of hot water now, I would be rid of the trail dust. Tell your stable hands that my packhorse may be cared for, but my stallion is not to be touched. Curiosity will get them killed and I will not pay gold to the family of a stupid child. We understand each other innkeeper?"

"Perfectly, absolutely sir. I will give the orders at once. Come along everyone. There is much to get done, and other quest to see too. Come along, come along. Oh sir, my name is Milty. Call on me whatever you need."

He bowed and moved his sweaty bulk from the room. Raven opened the window wide to air the room before going down the stairs to tend Chi and the packhorse.

Raven walked the animals around the building to the barn. The innkeeper was already there yelling at the stable boys about his horse. All eyes bugged as they got a close look at the prancing war stallion.

The mercenary growled softly into one pricked ear.

"Stop making a spectacle of yourself, you conceited ass. I do not need to peel some stupid boy off the bottom of your horseshoe in the morning."

Chi snorted and arched his neck, stepping higher, tail waving like a banner behind him. Suddenly his long neck snaked out and those talon sharp teeth snapped together. Everyone jumped in shock.

"You have been warned. He is trained for the battlefield. Don't go near him."

With that Raven led his animals into the barn. He unloaded the pack animal and gave her over to one of the stable hands. Then he went to the back of the barn, guiding Chi into an empty stall. Chi nibbled at Raven's hair and pulled on his leather shirt during the removal of his saddle and the necessary rubdown. The mercenary ignored him, too tired to appreciate the animal's joy at being out of the cold rainy weather. He did chuckle, however, when Chi's ears lay flat discovering his trough was to be filled with fresh oats instead of meat.

"I will feed you in the morning horse. I am too tired to deal with a nosy landlord this night." He was pushed into the side of the stall for his negligence and so removed himself rather quickly.

"Don't take your bad mood out on anyone I must bury in the morning Chi."

He noted the stable hands watching with some trepidation and knew he would sleep without worry. Raven hung his weapon's bag across his shoulders, picked up his travel bags and hauled the awkward load through the back door of the inn. As he suspected there were stairs to the left and right leading to the upper floors. Servants ran up and down, in and out of the kitchen, shifting around him like fish in a pond. The last of the servants were struggling up the two flights with buckets of water, possibly for him. Raven shivered at the thought of settling into hot soapy water. He walked in and put his bags on the bed.

On a low table near the fireplace was a cloth-covered tray. A kettle sat on a metal plate near the fire, steam rising from the spout. A chair with a high back had been placed before the flames. The warrior smiled to think of the landlord snatching it from the first floor rooms to grace a land less mercenary's dwelling. Raven was glad he hoarded the last fee. He could present himself well rested and there were enough silvers left to buy him new shirts and possibly new boots. A prosperous appearance would impress the uninitiated before tales of battles won.

The last of the servants bowed out of the room, so Raven barred the door. He stripped down and put his sweaty leathers and smelly cloak in the bag for that purpose. In the morning the cloak would be washed and he would clean and oil his leathers. From one pouch Raven sprinkled crushed green leaves over the steaming bath water. After a time, the smell of eucalyptus filled the room. Breathing deeply, the herbs eased the tightness in his chest. Illness dare not take hold when a job was at stake. He put a chunk of hard milled soap and a clean rag on the floor by the tub. Then filled his tankard with herbs from another pouch and poured the hot water over them leaving it to steep.

The platter on the table had thick slices of warm bread spread with, from the smell of it, goat cheese and a bowl of venison stew. He sat down immediately to eat, wiping up the last of the gravy with the bread. Drank the hot tea and finally relaxed.

Raven lowered his body into the tub and sighed with relief. Too tired to soak without falling asleep, he washed his hair and soaped the grime of his journey away. He rinsed with the two buckets left next to the tub and dried off with the bath sheets left by the servants. For a fighter, used to bathing in cold streams, this was luxury indeed.

Hair drying and braided once more, Raven stowed his gear under the bed, except for a short sword that looked like a big dagger in his large hands. It would lie next to him in bed. He blew out the candles, leaving his window partially open and the curtains pulled back. Satisfied with his precautions, Raven crawled into bed and sank gratefully into plump pillows and clean bedding.

Light filled the room before he woke. He pulled the bar from the door and went about the business of dressing for the day. Almost immediately the door opened and men began to empty the tub of the dirty water. Once empty they would take the tub down and wash it out. He congratulated himself once again that frugality was such a part of his life. Too many of his ilk drank and whored all their earnings away. They would not be eating well or present themselves clean and correctly attired.

He paid but scant attention to the servants once he was aware they posed no threat to him. But they were taking in as much as they could for gossip later. The tavern girls would love to know more about the big warrior that had pushed his way into Milty's Tavern and Beds. Like most they had known, his muscled body was covered with scars. One vicious burn marked his back from shoulder to buttocks. When he turned to watch another arrival deliver his breakfast, they noted he was not small in the place that mattered to wenches, but a ring of what appeared to be gold pierced it and his nipples!

Raven cradled his staff and balls into an odd quilted pouch and secured it by thin leather straps across his hips. He sat on the bed to pull on heavy stockings, wool breeches and boots. The tub was dragged from the room as he sat down to eat.

The landlord could be commended. He knew how to feed a hungry man. A half loaf of bread, a pot each of butter and honey, and hot porridge laced with nuts had been delivered. A metal platter held thick slices of ham, four boiled eggs and a serving of wild greens. He ate heartily washing it all down with another tankard of tea.

He finished dressing, putting on a thick wool shirt, his hunting knife and buckskin coat. He sat the tray outside the door and walked down the back stairs to the kitchen. Waving the cook over, he asked the woman if it was possible to purchase any fresh meat in town. She told him hunters came to the market during the winter. They went out everyday now because so many people had come to town. She gave him directions and he thanked her and went to the barn.

Chi stood with his head hanging over the stall door staring in Raven's direction. His black lips were drawn back, odd white fangs exposed and glistening with saliva drooling onto the floor. The hair on the mercenary's body stood up. He could only stare back. It took more than a moment to shake off the instinctive fear that gripped him. Chi could still scare him and he hated that fact.

"Stop glaring at me you devil. If my life is so bad, go back to the plains."

He physically shook off the shiver that raced down his spine.

"All right, I said I would get meat this morning and I will."

Chi jerked his head back, and then trotted the length of the barn. He butted Raven gently, nuzzling his neck chest and belly. Chi was, maybe, a little contrite. Raven shook his head, caressed the soft muzzle and scratched behind the horse's ears. Chi's forked tongue slipped around his wrists and flickered about catching his scent. The mercenary stepped closer and wrapped his arms around Chi's neck. For a time, they communed together in silence, the horse supporting his weight.

Raven did not understand the connection. He sometimes wondered if he felt anything at all. But for an undetermined moment he was just not "here" when horse and rider made good morning. He would have gladly avoided this morning's appraisal, however. As surely has the sun came up Chi would never hurt him, but then Chi was and was not what he appeared. Like a well-trained warrior, the horse kept him on alert. Life had taught Raven much, a friend today could be stabbing you tomorrow. What ability to trust remained to the man centered on his steed. Chi instructed him as well as protected.

"Come along. The cook says there is a market off the high road. If the meat is not fresh kill we will go hunting together."

Chi danced away, impatient to get moving. Raven left by the wagon gate, propped open to allow vendors to bring in fresh supplies. The horse paced him, eyes surveying his surroundings. Cooks and helpers were coming and going, some with wagons of fresh goods for the inns and taverns. Raven picked up his pace. He ducked into a side road and followed it until he came to a field separated from the buildings by a low wall. It was nothing to hop over. The hunters were here, sharing the wide grassy lot with the tents of itinerant merchants and a few farmers. Chi would choose and Raven would buy whatever he wanted.

The hunters were cleaning the site after a morning of butchering. They were surprised by the big man and horse appearing among them. Quickly enough they realized he was actually there to buy. Chi sniffed and nudged deer, mountain goat and even bear. His actions garnered more than a few comments. Raven was beginning to think they would have to hunt themselves, when another hunter rode in, animals still strapped to his pack horses. Some of the men heckled him for his late arrival. Chi immediately turned to follow him. The hunter looked over his shoulder at the pair and scowled. He stepped from the saddle and turned ready to fight if need be.

"Wha ya want. I ha wor ta da."

Raven frowned in return and growled.

"I came to buy meat. What else would I be doing here?"

"Humph. It loo lake na merchant."

"What I am is no concern of yours. I have silver. You are late and money has already been missed. Do I buy or take my money someplace else?"

"Na dress ye. Ha ta wa."

Raven looked to Chi. The horse was tugging at one of the carcasses.

"How much for that buck, now."

"I ga gol fa buck."

Raven laughed.

"By the time any cooks come back your meat will not be worth ten coppers. Sell me the buck. Two silvers and you don't even have to dress it."

"Sa silva loo silva."

Raven slipped the silver coins from his pouch and tossed them in the air. A dirty bloodied hand caught them. He turned away to help Chi pull off the carcass.

"Whoa tha. I ga it, sta has slabber on evathi!"

Raven stopped the man's advance with a big hand smacked against his chest.

"I will cut it down. You stay away from my horse."

The man wanted to complain further, but the irritated squint from those hard eyes stopped him cold. He watched closely, however, making sure they did not take what was not paid for. Raven cut the rawhide tying the legs together and heaved the carcass over Chi's back.

"Go beast and eat in private. I have clothes to buy."

The horse snorted and walked away from the hunters toward a distant stand of trees. Raven rarely watched Chi consume his kills. It was enough to see what he did to enemies in battle. After a meal there was no more than skin, skull and hipbones left. Pretty much all activity stopped when the men realized the horse was leaving and Raven was walking back to the center of the market.

Signs to ward off evil fluttered from one hand to another. Speculation would be all over town by the time torches were lit for the night. A Thanatu warrior and his stallion had come to Virgilia.

For the next two hours Raven enjoyed the market. He looked at everything twice, watched which stalls were frequented the most and listened to the conversations. Finally, he went in and haggled with a cloth merchant, buying yards of fine gray and black woolen to have shirts and breeches made. He carried it to a seamstress who took great delight in measuring his big body for the clothes. She was not young, but her long blond locks and bright blue eyes gave lie to her true age. Her nipples pressed against her coarse gown and she managed to, accidentally, rub her large breasts along his legs and back. She was happy to oblige him and flirted continuously. She smelled good, clean. It had been a long time since he had bedded a good woman. If he were not preparing himself for war he would have indulged her. Perhaps before he left for the fighting she would consider a tumble.

After leaving her shop, Raven purchased a yellowed bearskin. The fighter had never seen a white bear before. He returned to the seamstress and paid nearly the last of his money to have the skin cleaned. It would make a warm coat and be good cover in the snow. Satisfied, he returned to the inn. A coach was pulling out of the double gates, so he slipped into the yard.

"You, yes you. My horse will be coming back in a while. Make sure he does not have to jump the gate."

The stable hand gave him a confused look. Impatient Raven shoved a cooper into his hand.

"Do not lock the gate. My horse is coming back."

Still staring the man wrapped his fist around the coin and nodded.

Raven grunted in disgust. He spoke the local language fairly well. Perhaps the man was damaged in the head.

He shook his head in annoyance and went to relieve himself in the public houses behind the barn. Another gold coin would have gained him a room with a closeted chamber pot. Raven went up to his room, noting nothing was disturbed. He removed his coat and washed his face and hands in the cold water left from the morning. Before he was dry a knock prefaced the door swinging open. A maid this time, giving him the eye before she asked if he required her services. A sheen of sweat covered her face, neck and bosom. Dark hair slipped from beneath a dingy scarf. She already labored in the kitchen or the taproom.

"I will eat in the taproom now, two hours past sunset in my room."

"Inni tha morikin?"

He tossed her a copper.

"Nothing now, maybe later."

She smiled and shut the door. Milty did a good business here, but Raven was sure a copper would be her daily wage plus whatever she made sleeping with the customers. He would definitely not be sampling the wares.

The room was crowded. He drew a few stares, shifting past the people to gain the tables near the opposite wall. He was momentarily nonplussed. His intention had not been to intimidate. Never the less, the well-dressed patrons whispered and stared. A scowl, a glare convinced a few to go back to their conversations. Barmaids looked him over and hurried to serve customers so they could wait on him. One noticed he smelled very good and everyone knew he bathed the night before. A girl should not pass up the chance to bed such a fine looking warrior.

Milty rushed into the room, looked around and came right to him.

"Sir, forgive the intrusion. Your horse is loose. He jumped the gate into the barnyard and..."

"He jumped the gate? I gave one of your stable hands a copper to see the gate open for him. Raven eyed the sweaty innkeeper in irritation.

"I do not pour money down an empty hold."

"You paid one of my men to open the gate for your horse." Milty made it a statement rife with disbelief, attempting not to smile.

"Ask him yourself. I will have that copper back too. I paid gold to be here and you said my needs would be met..."

At that moment the girl from his room lurched against the table. The tray shivered and crockery rattled when she put it before him.

"Sor, me na rdy."

"No matter. Landlord is there something else you wish to say?"

"Your horse sir..."

"Is he injured?" Raven rose to his feet anger rising with him.

"No, no sir! As far as I know the animal is fine. I did not realize you knew he was loose about the town."

Raven sighed. All he wanted right now was to eat, not discuss Chi coming back to the inn.

"The animal is in his stall? He is not attacking your servants?"

"Yes and no sir he is indeed not attacking anyone."

"Well then leave me to my meal and fuss over someone else."

Raven sat down and lifted the lids from the bowls on the table. Milty attempted to speak again, but the mercenary's ugly scowl reminded him that other customers awaited his assistance. Raven relaxed and tucked into his food.

Conversation picked up when the patrons realized the big warrior was not going to rampage through the room. He listened to merchants complain about the dangers of hauling goods to the outlying estates and nobles worry the lord would strip their holds of the few soldiers they had left. Rumor had the raiders already moving on the borders.

'Why was the lord taking so long to move his soldiers? What was a ruffian ... owner thinking...won't stay here? How much longer...no money... raided... our people will starve. I heard...purse empty...rabble burned the manor...he was...Impossible...he is too large and...Wolves dragged them...married Rollo...no dowry... farther for game...more peasants...sickness in the lower town...heir killed...children taken."

After a while Raven realized he would hear nothing more of interest. Ale and wine topped off tankards and pitchers continuously, the occupants drinking to drown their woes. He pushed the table away and some of the people watched warily as he stalked from the room. His leathers still needed cleaning and his weapons sharpened. First he would go out and check on his recalcitrant steed. The stable boys scurried from his path. He dodged two arriving carriages and at least a dozen outriders. There was much shouting of orders, complaints from the richly appointed family and servants. Milty's shrill voice added to the din. The barn doors were wide awaiting the carriages and horses. The outriders would be sent to find lodging in the lower roads. A few nights in a dirty barn and tumbling with a diseased whore more than likely. He remembered his youth with distaste. When he first started selling his fighting skills there had been many nights in the lowest taverns, listening to coarse, sometimes violent couplings, vomiting and fighting. He shook off the memories with a shudder.

Chi didn't look up when he entered the stall. The beast was asleep, digesting the buck he consumed. His belly was a little swollen. It would take a couple of days before he was up to fighting speed. Then again, he would not need to eat like that again for at least a month, longer if they saw little action. Raven petted him, murmuring in the Thanatu tongue to assure the horse all was well. Before leaving the barn Raven gave his packhorse some attention, happy to see the sturdy little mare was resting comfortably and eating her head off.

The carriage horses were brought in and the carriages pushed into the shed next door. He went back and closed the stall door, lingering there until the new animals were settled. The leader of the outriders came in to be sure all was well and gave the big mercenary a long look. Raven ignored him. He was past the point that every petty challenge must to be met. His reputation as a fighter on the field was what mattered now. He grimaced as the man headed his way.

"Greetings to you warrior. I am Garst of Keb Hall. My master is looking for men to protect his holdings. If you are for hire you might consider. He pays well."

"I am here to sign at the hall with your lord. If the NorBlad are stopped your master will not have to worry about his lands."

"It has not been easy to get the nobles to band together. I know you speak the truth, but not many will follow Jerred's advice. There are some that believe he will give us up to the raiders. He came home with a fighter called Ullric and put him in charge of his troops."

"Humph. The name tastes of the north."

"Tis true. He is NorBlad and will not deny it. It is said a man will water the earth with fear before facing him. He is even bigger than you and fights with sword and axe. There are already men with him sworn to the lord. It is not easy to get good fighters when Jerred offers gold."

"No one would know the enemy like one of their own. There may be good reasons, but I will not ride with a traitor."

The guardsman glanced over Raven's shoulder.

"Your mount is well?"

Raven grinned.

"He just ate his fool head off and now must sleep off the effects."

A hoof struck the stable door with a bang, bouncing Raven's body.

He laughed out right and banged his fist against the door. An irritated snort was the last sound.

"Chi is very sensitive. I am sure he will bite me for the insult first chance he gets."

The other man laughed in the careful way one does when speaking to the mad.

"Well think on what I said. I need all the help I can get. My master can not find his own room let alone lead troops."

"Perhaps you should leave his service and ride against the enemy with Jerred."

"You are sure of yourself."

"I have seen what happens to men who hesitate. Their homes burn; their women are raped and murdered. The children are enslaved or raised by the enemy. Unknowing they raise sword against their fellows later on."

"Your family suffered this fate?"

Raven spat into the straw at his feet and jerked away from the door.

"I have no family." He snapped and stalked from the barn.

He was in his room, the door slamming behind him. Shame burned like the hellfire, which scared his back. Get of a slave, unwanted. Despised by the woman who bore him until the day he was beaten like a stray cur and hunted through the mountains for sport.

I am not that boy. I am not that boy.

Lost in the past, Raven paced. He was oiling leathers when reality returned. Hours later he packed the clean and supple clothes away. He pulled his Thanatu swords from the bag beneath the bed. He sat himself to the task of honing the thin blades and polishing the metal. Old leather was cut away from the grips. Two hours later the intricate pattern was repeated with fresh leather strips. After they were wrapped and packed away Raven sharpened his long sword. He oiled the scabbard and replaced the leather strap that belted it to his back. There was a soft knock at the door.

"Come."

The door opened to a different serving maid this time.

"A ha a speshal tre far ya b'man."

"And what might that be?"

He asked curtly and her smile slipped just a tad.

"Milty coo tani. Hi up lard ta sta. Ha poodin ina roost si a bee."

"Sounds good. Put it there. Here is a copper for your trouble."

"Hattie sa ya gi goo far 'elp. Ya goo ta Simi?"

Raven forced a smile and tucked the copper into the edge of her blouse.

"Yes I am good to Simi too. Now off with you before my food is cold. Wait do not bring breakfast tomorrow. I will be gone early and back late."

He nudged her to the door and lightly smacked her bottom. She giggled and swung her generous hips down the hallway.

He looked back at the steaming dishes and sighed. Seeing no other way to ease his mind, Raven closed the door and went down the back stairs crossing to the barn. He ignored the activity around him, going straight to Chi.

The animal was waiting, craning his neck over the door to watch him come. Raven opened the door with slightly trembling fingers. At the rear of the stall, shrouded in darkness, Raven wrapped his arms around Chi's neck and wished it all away...

He stretched and rubbed Chi down to thank him for, whatever it was he did.

The pain of the past was sometimes overwhelming. It could interfere with his work and that would get him killed. Chi had an investment in his future as well. The horse found hunting annoying, why else keep a human around?

Raven smiled again, this time in real amusement.

Chi snorted and butted him in the stomach. Raven laughed out loud as he fell against the wall. They pushed and shoved each other until Raven stood outside, grinning at his mount.

"In the morning I go to work the swords. I hope you will come."

He caressed the soft muzzle once more then went back to his room.

He ate slices of beef, gravy and roasted potatoes with a half loaf of fresh bread slathered with butter. A kettle on the edge of the fireplace bubbled so he prepared tea. When it was ready he sat down again eating the pudding Milty prepared. It was a soft cake like mass with currants and walnuts brushed with honey. In the chill weather, Raven was very grateful for the well-prepared food. The chances are he would not eat this good until he left the lord's service. He put the dirty dishes outside the door. A quick trip to the outhouse then he washed his hands and face before bed. After barring the door Raven stripped down and settled against the headboard. He honed the wide thick blade of his hunting knife. He owned three more, not to be used unless he broke this one. It was a frightening thing with flared ridges along the top for tearing and a wicked edge. It was so keen men laughed before their bellies sprang open and the entrails fell to the ground. In battle it was his last defense before fists and feet. He made sure it was spotlessly clean before returning it to the scabbard.

Tonight he would prepare himself as carefully as his blades. The Thanatu harvested rare plants in the southern most reaches of their kingdom to create medicinal oils. It was so rare Raven would need to petition to ever obtain more. He opened a box carved with ancient symbols. He could not read it and was not told what it meant. But he followed instructions precisely. He removed moist leaves from a pale brown cube. It had the consistency of chilled grease, but the fragrance always mesmerized him. He sliced a portion from it and put it in the tiny bowl setting it near the fireplace to melt. The remainder was quickly returned to its hiding place among his belongings. The gold rings in nipples and foreskin were removed and placed near him.

When the fragrance permeated the room, Raven placed the bowl on the table. First the braid was knotted at the back of his neck. He worked the warm oil into his body, beginning with the hands. He lost himself in the job, kneading heavy muscles until all the oil was gone. Replacing the rings he climbed into bed and was instantly asleep.

Raven was up and dressed before the sun crested the mountains. He carried the weapons bag across his shoulders. Chi was waiting in the stable yard, snorting and snapping at the cold air. He was silent on the walk to the forest edge where Chi broke fast two days before. Deep in the trees he found the perfect spot to practice. First he breathed in a required number of patterns. Soon his body followed, skimming the edges of the clearing as silently as possible. If the enemy would hear his movement, Chi would force him to start from the beginning. It was a slow acrobatic dance. The forest floor must be as air beneath his feet. Twigs must not snap beneath his weight, nor should his passing disturb branch or bush. Six times he repeated the moves, each time in a location chosen by Chi. Twice he was forced to start over. One turn completed clothed, one turn without.

Finally, the exercise moved to the center of the clearing. The combat rings were a pattern long set in his mind. With each blade he moved within the five rings, thrust, parry, leap, slash until the rings were tightly woven around his own body.

Seeking the serpent...

Wind and mountain...

Sippers at petals...

Bees and bear...

Serpent on water...

Maiden before the flower...

Each time Chi replaced the imaginary enemy so he parried sharp hooves and fangs. Four hours later he was still working, just a few bleeding cuts marking him. He would begin anew every time his guard slipped. They worked through the day, including the small knives stowed in the lining of his war bag and his hunting knife.

Bee to Blossom...

Hawk to Rabbit...

Serpent to Rabbit...

Cave Cat Strike...

When Chi seemed satisfied, it was well nigh the supper hour. The weapons were wiped clean. Raven followed Chi to a tiny rivulet of icy water tumbling down the mountain. Here he washed sweat and blood from his body. Raven ran back to the inn, Chi watching his back in the lowering evening.

The horse trotted into the barn, handlers and stable boys swerving from his path. Signs of warding disturbed the air behind him, some daring to stare after him. His stall was mucked out and fresh water and grain filled the bins. His system was still digesting so he would not need the oats. He sucked the trough dry though. Backing out of the stall, he spied a bucket and went to pick it up. Walking to one of the boys, he shook the bucket before him. Eyes huge, the lad took the vessel and filled it, twice more. Chi allowed the brave fellow to touch him. Just once. The snap of teeth sent the child running. It was the first time they heard the chilling hiss of Chi's amusement.

Raven stopped before climbing the stairs and peeked into the kitchen. The cook was yelling instructions, servants rushing about to carry out her bellowed orders. The smell of food made his mouth water. She finally noticed him and cuffed a serving girl in his direction. He spoke quickly and slipped a copper in her hand. Once in his room, the bags were put away. Stripping the coat and shirt off, Raven put a healing salve on his cuts and scrapes. He must perform better than today. There was a knock and the servant came in to put a tray on the table.

"Bring another kettle. It will snow tonight. I will want more tea."

"Shur ta bri it. Inni thin moa?"

"Nothing now, thank you." He gave her a lazy smile beneath lowered lashes. This one blushed all over and ran to do as he asked. Her reaction kept the smile on his face while he settled to his meal.

A large bowl of hot grain laced with wild onions, chunks of meat and greenery was consumed first. There were two roasted rabbits, bread and goat cheese. A covered tankard held strong black tea. He wondered where Milty obtained such a thing. He removed the ball and filled another tankard with water. Even used, the tea darkened his cup and filled the air with its scent. The last bowl held some kind of sweet fruit laced with dough and the faint scent of spirits. He ate this very slowly drawing out the pleasure of the fruit and spices on his tongue.

The girl tumbled in with a fresh kettle, and then refilled his pitcher and basin with the water remaining in the first one. Before she could slip away, Raven kissed her on the cheek. She blushed red and ran from the room. He could hear her embarrassed giggle from the back stairs passage way. He closed and barred the door. The remainder of the evening consisted of resting the body and mentally re-enacting every move of practice.

During sleep, his body twitched and rolled within the five rings.

For the next seven days, Raven left before sun up and returned in time for dinner. Muscles once again reacted fast as thought. He was marked less and less by the quickness of his mount. He was becoming oblivious to the cold and snow.

His last job had not required much. Guarding a merchant train from the midlands to their southern borders demanded only a good sword arm. It was best to be prepared in the event he would be required to use the more unique skills he had been taught. Word probably reached the lord that an Thanatu fighter was in the town. These people had never seen Thanatu, so there would be skepticism.

In truth the Thanatu were a diminutive people. They commanded unknown territories to the west. Invaders always wished they had not attempted to do so. Thanatu fought to the death. They never took prisoners and allowed none of their own to be taken. Thanatu could be expelled by their own, but never enslaved. They compensated for their size with a fighting art that required your soul. The body was a weapon and what they did with a sharp blade made them legends. It also fueled the rumors that they were rich beyond imagining. Why else would they fight like beasts to protect their lands?

Raven had been riding where the wind blew him when he chanced upon the fight. He erroneously thought of rescuing the women, but he only tipped the scale in their favor by his intrusion. Afterward they would grant him any wish. He thought, "to be able to fight so well". He was taken to their stronghold, compelled to labor through ten winters against his own ignorance and suspicion. His size was, at times, a disadvantage, but his strength and patience were important compensators.

Then Chi appeared outside his tent one morning...

Consciousness returned far from the stronghold. He slipped from the horse's back trembling with exhaustion. How he came there he did not know. It was a death struggle to get the horse to take him back.

He needed all his fighting skills to keep the beast from killing him. Severely wounded, Raven would not give up; he would not become that sniveling weakling that once hid in trash heaps. So he knew from experience what Chi could do to an enemy. He still wore the scars, still felt the poison boil his blood in nightmares.

There came the time when the wind carried the call of far places to him. The Thanatu would not hold him, but Chi could not go. They had never, in memory, left the western plains. It tore him inside to leave the horse behind, but he could not remain. That last morning, Chi turned on the warriors. He savaged everything in his path to reach Raven. The leader of the hold stopped the carnage. Did his people forget that "not horse" decided the rider and not the people? So Raven rode off with a blood splattered stallion and the spoils of his battles.

On the eighth day of his sojourn in Virgilia an individual in worn armor trotted down the hill to post a notice in the market place. Supplies had arrived from the south and Jerred was once again ready to hire. All interested report on the thirteenth day.

On the tenth day Raven went to the seamstress. His clothes were ready. He tried everything on and she made what adjustments were needed. She was not so intent on her work that he did not notice her continued appreciation. Once on the job, there would not be consideration for this pleasure. She said her name was Mabe.

When they were finished with the packing and exchanging of coin he did not leave. Other customers entered the tent. While she assisted them, Raven stripped off his clothes and lay down on the cot behind the heavy curtain keeping her living quarters from prying eyes. She did not pretend to be startled when she ducked back through it. Her shift dropped to the floor and he saw that his first impressions were not false ones. Her belly was marked with the signs of previous births and her thighs were heavy. She had strong forearms and her hands were lean.

When she settled her body over his, Raven gave up his disciplines to enjoy this one night. He suckled long at her breast, groaning around her nipples with pleasure when she stroked his staff with the same rhythm. She smelled like wool and wood smoke. Her skin tasted of soap and sweat. She met him strength for strength, arms and legs grappling to grip and squeeze. He rubbed her long blonde hair all over his sweaty torso. Finally he flipped her beneath him, raised her legs in the air and buried his face between her thighs. She shouted in surprised outrage, but couldn't break his grip. Not too long after, the woman was writhing and moaning. Her strong hands held his head in place as he suckled and licked the dusky flesh. When her juices were spread all over his face, she pulled him up and kissed him until his lips were bruised. He pulled back with a gasp for air and settling her on his thighs, pushed into her body. The ring caused more consternation, but he soothed her with kisses as the warm metal pushed inside, held rigid by his hard staff. It took a few strokes, but Raven determined her most sensitive spot and changed his stroke. She kicked wildly when she peaked, no sounds but her panting breath. He pulled out of her body and removed the ring, entering her again in the next motion. He put the ring in his mouth and sucked it while he drove into her slick passage. He let himself drown in her flavor and scent. The ring fell from his mouth when he spilled his seed in a flurry of deep thrusts. She went to sleep, exhausted.

She woke up to his tongue buried between her thighs again. Before the night was over, he took her three more times. He licked her everywhere, to her embarrassed delight. She even put his staff in her mouth, something she had never wanted to do before.

Morning found him holding her tightly, kissing her breathless. He shook her roughly to get her attention.

"Hear me woman. Do you read?"

"Enu ta ga far gold fa tradin."

"Good. Get you stick and skin."

She went to the front of the tent and returned fairly quickly with the   requested items. Raven sat on the ground near her small fire. He pulled his stain box from an inside coat pocket. He stirred the thick substance inside the box until it was smooth. With quick strokes, Raven marked the skin with a raven and the symbol, which meant "child". He stared at the woman for a moment, then drew the symbol for the Valley of Strong Waters. It was a place the Thanatu women went to give birth. The babes must swim when the umbilical cord is cut. The weak wash down stream to the sea. He thought this woman would have a strong child. In that event, he would know and see it cared for.

"If you quicken with child, send this to Jerred's hold. No one can read it but me."

"I ha goo tradin. No ne.."

He jumped to his feet and shook her.

"You will send word woman. I will not return to find my son cast off!"

Her eyes blazed with anger and she snatched her arm away.

"I ha boy I ha girls. I keep my yun uns. No cold no 'cast off'."

Angry tears filled her eyes and she pushed him. He grabbed her and with some struggle managed to press her close to his chest.

"Give over, give over. I ask forgiveness. I would leave gold to help if a child comes. You were not to be forgotten Mabe. I mean no insult to you. I did not want you to be alone, but I must go and fight the NorBlad."

She shoved against his chest again and spoke, her voice muffled by his coat.

"Fool ma, no lis to Mabe. Ha boy, ha girls...", she laughed until her shoulders shook, "they ha boys a girls. No ha woori, luf babes."

Raven pressed his face to her hair shaken that he believed her.

"If you say so Mabe. I will believe you. But I...I must know if a child comes. Promise you will send the word. It is important to me."

Mabe pulled away from him then and stared long into his pale eyes.

"Mabe see," she whispered, "Mabe kno, no woori gi sig ta Jerred."

He hugged her in relief and whispered apologies for shaking her and yelling. She laughed.

"Be ma allus yell. Alla ti noise. Soo ti ma yell li woman!"

She laughed at the look on his face.

"We will see who yells like a woman."

Raven laughed and tossed her over his shoulder. She was flat on her back and shrieking with laughter at the same time she attempted to prevent him from removing her shift again. Mabe was sleeping when he finally left, the last of his gold tucked in her hand. Other eyes in the market place noted his departure.

Some would not speak to Mabe for many days.

That night Raven demanded two portions of everything Milty served.

The maids graced him with sour glances. He reeked of sex. The satisfied grin on his face under scored the point, some woman had got him between her legs and it was not any of them. He fell into bed and slept like a stone until morning.

Raven was running to the forest with Chi snapping at his heels before the sun touched the roof of the highest building. He used all his stealth and patience for the next two days, now totally focused on obtaining employment.

The sun was up two hours when the timbered gates of the manor opened. A horn blew one long note and the impatient men and women seeking work as fighters trekked up the hill. There must have been near a hundred of them. Raven rode astride, his packhorse on a short lead. Chi kept a sedate pace. His occasionally snapping jaws keeping those on foot from crowding them.   There were a few others riding. The horses were in various states of care. Serious warriors and younger sons of the richer landowners rode strong and healthy mounts. The ill kept or sickly were owned by poor farmers or drunken louts. It was indeed a mixed lot looking for Jerred to lead them.

Armed men guarded the gates, the palisade a

mixture of thick timber gradually being replaced by large stones. They scrutinized everyone. The drunk and maimed were plucked from the crowd. It slowed down the procession, but it meant less time wasted once inside. It was nearly an hour before Raven passed through.

Across the wide yard a makeshift pavilion had been set up before the hall and outbuildings. Jerred's banner snapped in the wind above it, a pine tree covered by crossed battle-axes on a blue field. The manor was a one story timber building that reminded one of the plainsmen's tunnel halls. There were many doors, double and single along the front porch, some open for airing. Servants moved about attending the house and corralled cattle and horses.

Lord Jerred sat in a high backed chair, armed men standing to each side. Raven saw a young man, much younger than expected. His dress was subdued. A coat of bearskin and a dark brown silk shirt over woolen pants and sturdy boots. He was not yet into his full growth. The hands that griped the long sword were large against slim wrists. Brown eyes looked over the people with a steady gaze, earth brown hair tied back in a thick braid. Whether he could lead men was a different question.

Finally everyone was inside. Silence swept over the crowd. Jerred stood to address his people.

"I am Jerred, son of Rykk. The years have seen the NorBlad bring blood and starvation to our land. For years tribute was paid, the best of our land in the enemy's hand. My sister was given in tribute to be honored as wife. Yet the NorBlad brings blood and starvation to our land once again. My father is dead. Tribute is no more. My sister is dead. This bitter peace has ended. This year we go to the NorBlad and bring blood to their mountains. If you would defend, if you would fight, state your case and sign in blood."

The crowd roared their approval, the more so that Jerred paid in gold.

"We are well supplied with victuals and weapons. Many of you have your own. I ask those with the most experience to move to my right, the young and the homesteaders to my left. There is no shame if you must be taught, but shamed you will be to let your fellows down in battle."

So the crowd split in two with much reddening of faces for many. Once the crowd settled again Jerred resumed.

"I know you have heard that I have as my right hand Ullric, of the NorBlad. Hear me, it is so. Hear him, before you decide what to do."

From the shadows within the pavilion stepped one of the tallest men ever seen in any country. He was stripped to loincloth, buckskin leggings and boots. A wide band of leather strapped a heavily muscled chest to support the battle-axe on his back. Wide shaggy bands of snow bear hide, heavy with small silver rings, encircled his forearms acknowledgment of his personal kills in the way of the NorBlad. His hair was yellow, cut short and curling close to his skull. He was bearded. It too was tightly curled. Even his chest and arms were covered with curls of darker hair. His fierce green gaze swept the crowd and more than one person shivered beneath his stare.

"I am Ullric. I battled for the Wolf Pack as my father before me. Our pack leader took Grete, sister of Jerred to wife as was his duty. It came to be he spoke for the end of fighting and to trade with those below storms. Some came to think as he and spoke openly to the council of their thoughts.

Dedric feared the council would be swayed and end the raiding of these hills. He called the speakers of peace old women with water in their bowels. The council disbanded to speak again after this raiding time. Otto and Grete were murdered on the trail to the hold, though all were promised safe passage from council. Many pack mates died with them. Everyone knows that Dedric did this, but because he calls himself king and allied with filth, no one will stand. I bring the message of death to Jerred and to tell you Dedric will force all of my people to take arms against you. This winter will be as no other. He demands your names forgotten on the wind."

A woman stepped forward. Her voice was loud and strong.

"And how came you here and no lie dead with your fellows."

"Otto was my blood, to be obeyed even before the Dedric. He sent me to ride escort for one he thought Dedric would harm. Our charges were returned safely, to burning houses. We fought. We were hunted. No one would fight with us. Dedric made pact with Ottfried. Those I have known all my life now fear Dedric's alliance with Ottfried more than revenge of the betrayed or war with you. It is said he welds great magic. Ottfried worships the unspoken ones."

Gasps and exclamations rippled through the crowd.

"The oldest of us charged the last of the pack with this message. They died to cover our going."

Jarred stepped forward again.

"Now you understand why we must take up arms. This is no matter of raiding. Dedric must be mad to think he will control this Ottfried. They kill for gods, not gold. We must stand strong and stop this threat forever or our children will be buried alive by this abomination."

There was much conversation among the crowd. All this debate and speculation began to annoy Raven.

Chi nipped his boot when he wanted to ride forward.

"We will fight Jerred. We will fight."

The crowd began to chant and beat their swords on shields. Even the mercenary's shouted and waved their fist in the air. The noise did not impress Raven. Once on the battle field many of those shouting defiance would be pissing their pants and crying for their mothers if they had one.

The crowd eventually settled and Ullric spoke again.

"All of those experienced in leading troops stand aside. The scouts or those wishing to be, see Elika." He pointed to another big man with wild red curls standing before the pavilion.

Anyone with special skills waits to speak to Jerred and me. Archers you must exhibit your skill on the field this afternoon. These other men will direct you to where you need to be. Swordsmen will test your skill as well. Move quickly and tonight you will have your tent by the river and be rested for practice in the morning. You will be the last. We march north in two days."

Ullric's men moved quickly and the majority of the people were lead to the riverbank behind the manor. They would participate in sword and archery exercises to determine their skill. Those with the most experience would find themselves teaching others, and or in charge of a unit.

Raven had no desire to lead anyone. He was versed in the use of various weapons. They could scout and track for game or the enemy. Mostly they could fight. He had been doing so since the first day he fought another child for moldy scraps and was beaten for it. Though he had never been north farther than he was now, Raven knew they could traverse the terrain quickly and spy on the enemy when the time came. And it was not his way to expose his abilities for all to see.

Jerred sat on a low stool and listened to the warriors relate their past experiences. From time to time he wrote something on a skin or read from ones presented to him. His eyes kept returning to the dark haired man at the back of the crowd. He was taller than most and well mounted. He dressed in black and wore a sword strapped to his back. His eyes scanned the area constantly. His vigilance had not relaxed at all. The young man contained his curiosity. He must be sure of the twenty or so that remained before him.

Eventually he dismissed the group to the field to await assignment. Some of the names he knew by reputation. After talking to Ullric a decision would be made.

The warrior finally stepped down from his horse and approached. His eyes were a very unusual pale gray, his gaze sharp. He inclined his head to Jarred in respect for his position in lieu of the courtly bow some of the nobles displayed.

"I am called Raven. This is Chi who battles at my side. We are Thanatu."

"It is said Thanatu are like shadow and cannot be seen by ordinary men. There are none so skilled with blades as they."

"Only those claimed by "not horse" may call themselves Thanatu. I was adopted when taken by "not horse". You have probably heard many lies as truth about my people. It is said you pay in gold. I have come."

"Do you have any to recommend you? Where have you fought before coming here?"

Raven reached inside his shirt and tossed four folded skins to Jarred. Once opened, Jarred read of the warrior's last employment, with the merchant vans to the south. Another related the death of raiders harassing a small holding who had lost their lord. It said he went in the night and that morning all were dead. He would not stay and marry the widow.

A noble and his captain related the day the walls of their holding were breached by opposing forces. Raven's arrival turned back destruction when he sliced through the troops, his swords flashing like lightening and the monster he rode ripping men apart with fangs like a mountain cat. The last was a list of former employers going back many years, even to the southern barrens. Jarred was taken aback. Surely the man standing before him was not that much older than himself.

"This is an amazing record. You are widely traveled."

"I have not been further north than this before. I dislike the cold and endless rain, but I have the skills you need to find and destroy your enemy. Among you are none with skill at dealing death as Chi. My price is one thousand gold to remain until death or the end of the campaign."

"Your price is steep, too steep for my bags."

"You are getting supplies and coin from the nobles of the midlands. Many of the soldiers already in your employ are sent by their lords, not for gold. You can afford me Jerred and you can believe these testaments. Some of those names you know."

"I must think on this. Go to the river. Tonight I will welcome you into my home. We will tell you then."

"Good enough. Keep those for now. Speak to others. My name is known more to the south than these hills and there are warriors here that know me."

Raven walked away leading the horses. He stood for a time looking over the sprawling camp. A few hundred resided along the banks of the tumbling river. A small herd of horses grazed. The sounds of clashing steel on steel rang in the air. Arrows from longbow and short punctured straw stuffed targets. People shouted instruction and curses, intent on their duties. Raven skirted the far edges of the ground. He found a place amid the forest and pitched his tent. It blended with the dark trees and was not easily seen. He unloaded the packhorse and hobbled her, then rubbed both animals down. He stripped down and sat on the grass and began his breathing exercises. Soon he drifted away, Chi standing guard.

Ullric stood at the side of Jarred's chair. He looked carefully at all the people coming into the room. These were the seasoned, with reputations to go with the hard eyes and scars they bore. Some had been sent by those wishing to support Jerred but many for the lure of gold.

There were women among the group. Some were welders of long and short sword. Some were small in stature hailing from the west. These were considered the best archers. They were Lua. Their strange repeating crossbows and longbows were made from woods that only grew in their country. Two captains were present, representing a troop of fifty. Jerred said he was very lucky this fight captured their attention. These women swore allegiance to no one but once paid to fight, their deadly skills were not turned from the enemy even if the cause was lost. It was said that a survivor would continue to harass the victor for years until she joined her sisters in death. They fought from horseback as well as fortified walls.

The western lands seemed rife with mysterious fighters of strange abilities. Ullric snorted in disgust. He heard tales, he would see them fight before he believed any of it.

The noise level faded slightly when the tall one entered. Raven was the name he gave himself. Right now the name fit. Ullric noted his black attire, even to his boots. He took off a buckskin coat, handing it off to a servant. He slipped along the outer wall of the room, then Ullric lost sight of him. He appeared again speaking to one of the archer captains. She was laughing and gripped his arm in obvious happy recognition.

Jerred entered the room and the babble of voices stilled. The young man went to his place at the head of the table.

"Sit down and fill your bellies. There will be time enough for talk and decisions."

Servants scurried into the room, loaded with heavy platters of meat, mostly venison and beef. Big bowls of wild greens appeared with roasted potatoes and onions. There were thick loaves of coarse bread and goat cheese. Pots of honeycomb were placed along the table.

Hands and blades flashed about the table as trenchers were loaded. Ullric's eyes were drawn again to the dark one. Unlike most, he speared his food from the bowls with a small knife. He sliced everything into smaller pieces, and like the archers, ate from the blades. It attracted some attention. Perhaps the Thanatu and Lua had closer ties than anyone suspected. He seemed younger now, sitting in animated conversation with women that usually kept to themselves. He was cuffed about the head more than once. The women were diminutive by mountain standards, the tallest not reaching Raven's shoulders. They always dressed in tanned hides with a woven leather chest protector strapped on. They were brown as the hides they wore from life in the open and wore their hair shorn close to the head.

Soon the meal was ended and the table cleared. The dark one restricted himself to water, though the archers helped themselves to the rich wine Jerred served. Ullric spoke from his place at Jarred's right.

"All of you are obviously serious fighters and many known to one another. Some have demanded much gold for their services. I question the amount of coin you expect."

Raven answered from his place.

"I know you question my price, Ullric. I am not known to you. The Lua know me. I have raised blade against them and fought at their side. It is the way of such as we. I charge for Chi and myself. The Thanatu would not insult "not horse" by treating them like pack animals. When I fight Chi fights with me. It is the way of my people."

The hair along Ullric's spine stood up.

"So you say this animal is one of the fabled stallions. How do we know this is true? It is said even the Thanatu are rarely seen riding such a beast."

"People say many things."

Raven came to his feet. He lifted the sword harness over his head and laid it before him. The Lua captains stood and assisted him in pulling the black wool tunic over his head. The gold rings flashed in the torchlight. He walked the length of the table and stood before Jarred. Raised sickle shaped scars marred chest, across his shoulders and upper back.

"The "not horses" take you far from the stronghold. Perhaps it is sorcery, I do not know. Night brings flashing teeth and sharp hooves. Do you fight or run? Do you survive days, months? I cannot tell you. Either choice is death. The venom is acid in your blood and your screams are the only thing you hear. Few are taken, even fewer return. If you do not ride you die. I am here with the skills of two. I can leave with the same."

He turned away.

Out of curiosity Jerred asked, "What of the scar on your back? You were trapped in a fire?"

Animation disappeared and Jerred looked into flat dead eyes.

"Hellfire."

Some at the table were shocked by the declaration. It was said to be created by sorcery and once ignited could not be put out. Only the richest and most ruthless of the lords had been reputed to use such heinous devices. When one of the most notorious lost control and destroyed his own holding, the midland lords banded together and made using hellfire a reason to call a death sentence.

Some of the occupants of the table could see the twisted knotted flesh across the young man's back and marveled he survived, others scoffed at the story.

Raven returned without hesitation to his place. He shrugged into his tunic, lifted the sword over his head and sat down. The room was silent. Speculation and legend had been clarified to some extent. Even the Lua had not known how he came to ride Chi.

Ullric would not be deterred.

"What is so special about this animal, other than an inclination to bite and a questionable devotion to you."

Raven glared at him.

"Chi is with me because he chooses to be. Enemy fleeing before us will not escape to take word. If there are suspected traitors among us he will know. If you wish to know your enemies plans, send us."

"You say he demon man? No horse can do these things. They cannot think as men."

"You believe what you must," Raven responded to the man across the table, "we do what I say we can. Chi is no daemon he is "not horse". We are Thanatu."

"Why is there hesitation? We know him, have done our best to target him in the past. Big as he is, our arrows never touch him. Only Thanatu can do this. He wears the truth on his body."

Before Ullric would speak again, Jerred intervened.

"I for one, would see what you could do. The reports you gave me were fantastic."

"I am hired because I can do what must be. I do not give exhibitions. I am not a performer in the market. It is not the Thanatu way to draw steel on a man unless we kill him. Remember that before you challenge, any of you."

His cold stare swept the room. Many signed against evil beneath the table.

"I mean no offense...Raven. You are first of your people among us. I would know more."

"I take none Lord Jerred. I understand your hesitation and will abide by your decision."

With that remark Raven turned his attention back to the conversation with the Lua. It disconcerted Jerred to be dismissed so abruptly. He took a moment to consider, however. Ullric was watching the warrior with an incredible scowl on his face.

"You think him insolent, Ullric?" Jerred spoke softly for his ears only.

"Look how big he is. People of the west be not tall and the Thanatu supposedly smaller still. He must be from the eastern mountains. You say the rabble that lives there are nearly as tall as NorBlad and no one I have seen in our travels have eyes like clear water."

"Even if that is true, he has plied his trade in the midlands and southern lands for many years. His skins are old and my scribe says they are not false. I do not think Dedric would have spent what gold he has to buy this one to spy on us. Your people rarely travel further than these mountains. Who would know how to find such as he?"

"I no longer know what Dedric thinks or does. A mad sickness has taken his brain. He would do anything to insure victory. Mercenaries are easily bought for silver as well as gold."

"Then there are none with us that will stay to fight Ullric and we are doomed."

The blonde warrior snorted in disgust. The boy was right enough about that. The southern most nobles would send gold, grudgingly, and supplies but not fighters. Some did not believe that a few worshipers of the old ways could pose so great a threat. The people at the foot of these mountains realized the danger and their people were here, for little pay and to protect their homes. Jarred and he fought for revenge. He would wipe Dedric from the earth with his last breath if need be.

"If you insist I can not stop you Jerred."

"Peace Ullric. I would not have a rift between us over this. If he can do as he says, we have an edge. Watch him. Ride at his side if you must, but give this a chance. It could win us the war."

Ullric turned his brilliant green gaze to the youth.

"You are a bold and daring leader Jerred. Let it be as you say. I will watch closely."

Jerred flushed under the compliment and set back in his chair. Except for the Thanatu, they had quickly decided what men to use at the front and who to hold the rear line. Once they moved out, the town would shield itself for the coming winter and be prepared to evacuate if all was lost. He stood to announce the assignments. It was handled quickly and the responses were without dissension.

"Raven, I would speak to you in private."

Raven inclined his head. The Lua fighters spoke to him before they walked out. It surprised everyone to hear his laughter when he dodged their swinging fists. The women were singularly dour and conversation outside the troop was rarely heard.

But it was the cold forbidding mask Jarred looked

on when the warrior turned to face them.

"We will hire you Raven of the Thanatu. If you can infiltrate the camps of the advanced forces so we know what to expect, it would be worth every coin and more to us."

"You need pay no more than my fee. War leaves many bellies empty regardless of the winner. Your people will need what you have left."

"Well spoken. Then I agree to your fee."

Jerred held his hand out and after a moment's hesitation, Raven took it in his. He did not squeeze but allowed it to rest for a moment. Jerred noted the Thanatu's palm had the thick calluses of a seasoned fighter. Jerred shook it and thanked him again.

"Sit. I would you go before us, not just to scout but to spy on the rabble that is already headed our way. These are not Dedric's true fighters, but bandits he has sent to raid. It is the reason for suspicion. We don't know how he managed to gather such a group since NorBlad do not travel beyond our borders. Someone had to send them word, pay or promise them spoils to have them come against us. Ullric will go with you."

Jarred waited for some protest and none was given.

"He knows the land and the hiding places of these men. It will make your job easier. Get back to me as soon as possible with your information."

"It will be as you say. I can leave now if you wish

it. I need only strike the tent and leave my pack horse with your hustlers."

Jerred looked to Ullric.

"Give me two hours. I have orders to give and gear to stow. You may leave all you will not take with my men. I have my own supply train. It will be safe."

"One thing. Lord Jerred, there is a woman called Mabe from your town. If she should come with a written message for me have it sent to the field. I would know this news. It concerns matters private, not your war. It is important."

Jarred studied his face for a moment and nodded.

"I will leave the instruction. It will be done as you say. Is there anything more to be done?"

"I say this to you both. You know this land and I must trust you guidance in this. Once we reach these camps, do not attempt to follow me. Your people walk like thunder through grass and I would not get my throat cut because of heavy feet."

Ullric frowned at the remark, but held his peace. He would follow and if this one spied for Dedric, then he would die.

"It will be as you say Raven. Be off you two. The rest of us will be behind you. We make first camp near Rayna Pass."

Jerred watched the men leave the hall. Ullric may not trust the strange fighter, but then again many said

Jerred was a fool to trust Ullric. No one else had seen the hopeless grief that burned in the blond giant's eyes. No one else would understand the depths of his hatred to come to an enemy after his people were dead and sundered by fear.

The old teachings had only disappeared beneath the ground where it was said they started. He for one would burn everything before leaving it to those bringing the old poison. The followers believed in human sacrifice. Victims buried alive, death by madness and starvation. He shuddered at the thought. It was time to take charge and get to the business of war.

Raven and Ullric separated at the back gate. Advised where to find the Wolf leader's wagon, Raven went to strike his tent. He changed his boots to the soft buckskin he wore for silent work. The coat was packed away. One travel bag held another woolen pair of black pants and shirt, the wool blanket he always carried and a small healing kit. Travel cakes were placed inside. Made from fruit, smoked meat and fat, the cakes were years old. It took much work of jaw muscle to wear them down. If he could not hunt, or was wounded they would be sustenance until safely back to the main camp. He took the last of Milty's good bread and sliced beef wrapped in tanned hide. He packed his heavy sword. For this job he would need the three light blades of his people. They were very slim, each progressively shorter than the others. He put an extra hunting knife in his bag and slipped the one he wore at his waist inside one moccasin. Extra small blades stowed easily in his bag. He was ready.

"Well Chi, it is time to earn our gold. The one called Wolf is to spy on us as we do the enemy. What do you think about that, horse? He is NorBlad, yet we are the ones they fear."

Chi only shoved him in the chest to get scratched behind the ears. If he cared at all about the state of affairs he kept it to himself. When he wanted to, Chi could play just a horse very well. Raven sighed and stepped in the saddle.

By the time Elika, Ivo and Noak received their orders and Ullric was packing, the dark one arrived. He handed over his belongings and the pack mare to Noak without a word. Ullric saddled his horse and put his bedroll across the saddle. In the dim light he could see the man was packed as lightly as he. He stepped into the saddle and headed for the trail. Raven followed without a sound.

The moon came up and they kept to the trail most of the night. Just before dawn, Ullric rode into the trees. He was not ready to rest yet. The quicker they found the bandits, the sooner he could see this Thanatu in action. It was strange that in all the hours they rode, the man had not spoken once. Whenever Ullric looked back, he appeared to be sleeping or checking out the countryside. Anyone else would have attempted to converse.

The sun was up three hours when Ullric called a halt. He watched when Raven pulled the saddle and allowed Chi to roll in the lush meadow grass. He pulled a rag from his pack and rubbed the animal down, then checked his hooves. He spent sometime talking in a strange tongue. It reminded him somewhat of the Lua's speech. It was obvious he had great affection for the animal. To Ullric's people a horse was stolen to fill one's belly or escape if needed. He turned his attention to filling said belly now. From his pack he took bread and cold meat, washing it down with water from the rivulet that rushed downhill to join the many rivers and lakes below storms. Raven came over and sat across from him. He ate swiftly and silently. Ullric looked up to find Chi creeping across the meadow. Raven grinned suddenly and looked over his shoulder.

"It will not be easy to steal when another is looking at you bright one."

Chi snorted and snapped at Raven, then boldly walked over nosing into his food.

"You should go hunting if you want meat. This is cooked and you know it. Stop. Stop I say." He snatched the packet away from the horse's questing mouth. "You do not want it and I will not have it wasted. Stop showing off."

The horse dodged the heavy fist aimed his way. He whinnied at Raven and ran across the open ground, kicking up his heels like a young colt.

"Bring back a rabbit for me great hunter." Raven chuckled momentarily forgetting about the man staring at him.

"I heard your horse eats meat. That is an unnatural thing."

Gray eyes narrowed to slits.

"Chi will not eat you, nor any man. His own kind yes and any other four leg is considered food. In this land he does not prey on the animals we keep to ride and to provide food. All other free life in the forest is his prey."

"You talk to it as if it understands you."

"He does. I do not know how or why. I rode him back to the stronghold and the Thanatu were amazed. I was not of them and yet he came for me. I only know I had to make him take me back, perhaps because he wanted to kill me so badly. I could feel it."

A cold shiver raced over his skin remembering that time of slashing hooves and tearing fangs. Being held down while slow poison was injected into his body. So weak and crazed with pain he prayed for death, put never voiced it, determined not to beg some demon spawn for his life. Never again to beg for anything.

Ullric watched his face. Although the words were matter of fact, the eyes were wide in remembered fear and an unbearable loathing.

"Then why did you not kill it. Why do you keep it." Raven laughed until he wiped tears from his eyes.

"You do not understand. I am his, he is not mine." The NorBlad looked on him in silence.

"I can not raise a hand to harm him. For the first time in my life I was worthy. For the first time I truly belonged. We are Thanatu, we are one."

"I heard you were mad. Now I am sure of it."

"You will see when the fighting comes. Chi has saved my neck more than once. On the battlefield he is the demon people think him."

"Humph. Well we should sleep. I want to move during the nights while the moon is high. Three days ride maybe another and we should find our bandits."

"Will Dedric strike at another place while Jarred chases bandits?"

"Not likely. He thinks these people sheep. It would not occur to him that I would dare seek Jerred. He may believe me burned on the pyre I made for my family. By the time he hears we are moving to face him, his only choice will be to meet us. He will expect the usual timid men guarding the borders, not an army of hundreds. The NorBlad have not changed in thousands of years. When the seed took root, Dedric crushed it."

Ullric's face was twisted with bitterness and pain. Raven recognized that look. It was his face many times over the years. He shook off memories and wrapped himself in his blanket.

"Sleep then. Chi has not gone far and he will keep watch."

"I would be foolish indeed to put my neck in a horse's keeping."

Raven did not comment. He was asleep. Ullric shook his head in disbelief. He was riding with a mad man and a careless one at that. He rested his back against a tree.

He was still alert some time later when Chi appeared like smoke in the meadow. The horse trotted over to Raven, sniffing and poking at the sleeping man. Satisfied with whatever he was doing, the animal lay down next to him. Horses were rarely off their feet. Ullric wondered if something was wrong.

Then Chi stretched his neck over Raven's body and looked at him. He could not break the gaze and unease wiggled up his spine. A forked tongue flicked out in his direction and that sight mesmerized Ullric. So it is true...yet it could not possibly be...What was it?

His fingers twitched and shoulder muscles tensed. Then the black muzzle pulled back and he saw, not the yellowed square teeth of any other horse, white sharp looking...fangs...What was it? What was it? Ullric was helpless. He could not stop looking. Those eyes, hunger...madness...

A blink, and Ullric was released. He collapsed, panting and body trembling. He could not reach for his axe, his arms refused to work.

Was the young warrior be-spelled as he was? Would this thing turn on him one day?

Only the eyes of a horse looked back at him now. The animal nuzzled at Raven's head and the warrior rolled over with a grunt. Ullric was suddenly exhausted. Try as he might, he could not stay awake.

"It is time we moved. Are you going to sleep all night?"

Raven's voice shook him from a deep dreamless sleep. He glared at the younger warrior. Anger simmered bitter in his belly. He had been afraid.

"I am always ready."

He gave Chi a baleful glance and stalked away to saddle his horse. Raven looked at his friend studiously nipping at the grass.

"What did you do Chi? He is afraid now. We have a job to do and now I must worry that he will try to kill you? You could have left well enough alone."

Chi just snorted. Ullric had already disappeared in the trees. Raven stepped into the saddle and Chi followed the warrior's path without hesitation.

They rode through the night and the next day. Chi did not falter and Raven knew to sleep whenever the urge hit him. They were well into the higher elevations when Ullric finally called a halt. He did not speak, just saw to his very tired horse and went to sleep. Raven followed suit.

The next two days were the same, a silent ride into the mountains, an occasional angry glare in Chi's direction.

It was part way through the fifth night when Ullric signaled a halt.

"We have come near a place well used in the past. Some of the pack leaders may be here already."

He quickly pointed to rock formations and tree growth that marked the suspected camp further up the mountain.

"If I am discovered do not expose yourself," Chi snorted, "leave me. I have gotten out of worse."

"I should go with you." Ullric asserted.

"You would make too much noise."

Raven pulled the braid around his neck apart. While the blond one watched in grim silence, he platted it again with small blades intertwined. He pulled the saddle from Chi's back and deftly tucked it and his travel bag out of sight in the boughs of a pine tree.

"I know what to do NorBlad. I will return with what you need to know."

And just like that he was not there. Ullric looked frantically around. The man disappeared into the dark like a wraith. He shivered, Chi's head was turned in his direction, although he could not see its eyes in the dark. Defiant, Ullric dismounted and secreted his horse in the deeper shadows. He pulled his axe from the scabbard and slipped away, moving as quietly as he could. It would be humiliating for Raven to catch him. It took hours of careful stealth before he found the first guard and managed to slip past him. This high up, the bandits would believe themselves safe. No one below the storms had ever dared this close to the pass and their territory even during the last tribute talks.

"So..."

He spun around, the axe slicing through air.

A blade sliced into his chin.

The blade sank further, he realized it was Raven.

"Tor...!"

His hands fell away. Am I mad, is this not what I came to prove?

The blade was gone.

Ullric listened, hard. The forest was undisturbed. He looked all about, now unsure if he should proceed. Blood dribbled onto his chest and he dabbed at the wound. It hurt like the very devils. The blade actually stabbed just back of the bone under his chin. It was deep but did not pierce his mouth. The seconds it took to realize, if Raven wanted him dead he would be, shook Ullric to his core. He moved so fast!

Damned fool NorBlad bastard! Did I not say let me work? Damned fool! And where on the demon plane were you damned horse?!

Raven settled in the branches of a thick pine. He needed to get back into the mindset to leave these raiders alive. He came for information and his ally tried to kill him. The urge to kill, unchecked, would not give Jerred what he needed. He inhaled slowly...

pine needles shushing in a cold breeze...arm...faint sensation...burn from the sap... across his back... bark... itching...

Raven dropped to the ground fading into the night, Ullric still standing beneath the tree.

All his life Ullric made decisions and plunged ahead. Now he could not decide whether to go back or follow. He clenched his jaw and the cut opened wider, bleeding worse. A trail back to them if Raven was chased off the mountain. Angry and not a little embarrassed, Ullric turned back toward camp, skirting wide around the guard he bypassed before.

His body was slick with sweat when he got back, only to find Chi, standing in the same place apparently asleep. Lightening blast him!

Ullric moved quickly to his bedroll and got the sealer. He poured the powder into his palm and spit, stirring with his finger. He carefully packed the wound until it began to harden. A little water cleaned blood from his chest and neck. Uneasy, but resigned, the man stretched out beneath some brush to wait.

The wind picked up, the pine boughs whispering in response. Raven listened from the edges of a camp. If this was an advance of bandits, they were awfully disciplined. The camp trailed up the mountain. Horses and weapons were in the center, twice guarded. How strange. Perhaps they were worried about deserters?

He slipped easily past the perimeter guards into the camp proper. Things were unusually quiet, no drinking, no laughter. Conversations were whispered, furtive glances flashed in the firelight. The bandits were easily identified by their ragged garments and sometimes rusted weapons, but there were also well-muscled warriors with gleaming metal at their backs. Their pale skin was streaked with some dark matter and when they passed men signed against evil or groveled like dogs. These must be the followers of the unspoken ones. Had Dedric sent them to make sure no one deserted or would they strike at the young leader that had risen among the mountain dwellers? Both groups avoided morose curly haired warriors with ringed bands at their wrist and no weapons! Questions...he needed to get closer.

...he wrinkled his nose. Here, dead? More alert he

stood in the shadows. A warrior passed, intent on some mission. A breeze brought the stench of rotting flesh to his nose. He stifled the gag reflex and faded away. He ran ahead of the man following the awful smell. Then he heard it, moans. Drifting closer, careful...

Squealing, rotting flesh and and an endless keening...

The piteous sounds rose from the earth, from a mound of dirt and stone. People, buried alive!

Bile filed his mouth. He fled, running silently, quick as a deer down the mountain. He stopped twice to gag, staggering.

Ullric had not been able to sleep. He lay in the dark waiting as the hours past. Suddenly, it snapped to attention then disappeared! Startled, angry, the warrior charged into the brush after the animal. To the devils with them both he would not be left in the dark!

He moved as quietly as he could, but was brought up short by snapping fangs. Peering past the looming menace, he could barely see a huddled figure on the ground. Had some drunken fool from the camp...

Chi moved, blocking his sight. A hiss like a knot of snakes made him flinch back, then realization, Raven had returned. If he was wounded, surely...

Chi stopped his advance once more, the long neck snaking out to strike.

"Damned to you. I would help if he is wounded!" I

must be insane. I am talking to a...

"Tell me," a harsh choked whisper, barely heard over the wind, "tell me what manner of beast these, people buried alive. NorBlad, tell me. What are you?"

Ullric spit on the earth and signed against evil.

"No one of these are NorBlad, but spawn of some sickness from beyond the walls of ice. So I was told as a child. I do not know what they believe, I do not care. Before Dedric did this thing, they were killed on sight. To harbor one brings the poison to many. They are here then?"

"Bandits, your people? On the mound, weapons. No warrior should do to another this thing. To die for some purpose, in battle..."

"Raven, are you wounded? Do they know we are here?"

"They do not know."

"Are you wounded? The devils take you man, or you wounded?"

"... ..."

"Raven." Ullric twitched, and jerked away when Chi's snapping teeth just missed him.

"The devils take you then!" The enraged warrior stomped away, disregarding the army that loomed above him. Demon spawn on the mountain and demon spawn in my camp the world is coming to an end.

Raven stood and wrapped his arms tightly around Chi's neck.

"I would make them fear. What power do they have, that strong warriors cringe before them, that a lord would sell his people just to keep raiding a few small holds. I, I ran away. I was made sick, and we have seen strange and frightening things. We have spilled much blood, but I could not do this to the one I hated above all living. What god demands such tribute?"

Chi just snorted and nuzzled at the face and hair of his charge. Eventually Raven fell into that place of emptiness where nothing was. Chi was his anchor and protection. All he needed in the world.

Ullric sat with axe across his knees. It bothered him that he could not confirm if Raven was wounded. He was afraid of the thing. By the gods, he was a coward. That devil Raven rode would let him die one day, just to keep him be-spelled. Ullric shivered remembering their conversation, joy and terror on his young face, speaking of being worthy of some god's venom spat to earth. What life had he led that would make this frightening connection a precious thing? What had losing his home done to him, that a man may lay wounded and he too frightened to best a...a...devil's take him!

Ullric leaped to his feet and plunged back into the brush to find them.

His axe was poised to strike when he came upon the duo in the dawning light.

Horse and rider leaned into each other, appearing asleep. Raven's hands clutched at the long mane, his face invisible in the hair. Chi stood, head down over the man's back. After the first shock, Ullric noted they each took breath the same as the other. For the moment he could only watch, amazed. Then Raven's fingers twitched and moved in a stroking motion. Chi lifted his head and nuzzled the man. They moved apart and stared at each other. The man's face was innocent, like a youth not yet tried.

Raven began to speak. The low murmur sounded like a chant. He began to rub the thing down as if it had run for hours. Occasionally, the animal would nuzzle the warrior, gently butt him in the chest or pretend to nip at his backside. Ullric saw a playfulness, a regard he did not expect. Once again, he was at a loss. What was this...thing between them? This was not a man driven by fear of his companion. This was not the beast that drooled and watched him like ten starving devils.

Reluctantly he put the axe back in its place. Chi was gazing at him with soft horse eyes. In the morning light he could question the malevolent stare of the nights just past. Raven finished his ministrations and turned to the other warrior.

"Ride to Jerred and tell him what I have seen. Tell

him there are nearly a hundred men here. Tell him, tell him we will harass this rabble as they come. It may interfere with Dedric's plan if he would meet them now. We will see if they know more. If this many are here, how many could Dedric have waiting or moving to another point?"

"Even with Ottfried's men, no more than Jerred has, probably much less. There are few of us and now that Dedric has eliminated the strongest families," he shrugged. "Those that follow the unspoken ones are fewer still. This is why it makes no sense. While we raided here, even when Jerred's people did fight, none of the lowlanders ever interfered. My people are renowned for berserk rages. We are feared and hard to kill. But even we cannot fight the whole of the middle ranges."

"Go now. The faster you get to Jerred, the sooner this will end."

"Even with...Chi. You cannot fight off an army."

"I don't intend to. We will make enough trouble to slow them down. I, I cannot free the..."

"No, they are dead mad men. We can clean this place with good steel and fire."

"Fire..."

"Leave some filth for me to clear away. I will return with Elika and the others."

After that remark Ullric turned away.   Raven

listened for his arrival where his horse was tethered. Ullric would ride until the animal collapsed. Raven thought that a stupid waste of horseflesh. He put the blond warrior from his mind and slipped back up the mountain.

That night fire broke out in the camp. A number of tents burned and in the confusion a few men deserted. Some of the horses became ill in the morning. No reason could be deduced. Guards vanished at nightfall. A through search revealed nothing. Angry men accused each other until scattered fighting erupted. Whatever ailed the horses spread to the men the next day. Nearly a quarter of them could not raise their heads, let alone stand in battle.

Then the sacrifice was tainted. The heads of the missing guards were discovered the next morning atop the sacrificial mound. There was only silence from within. Eskil, leader of Ottfried's men went mad. The forest was searched again, men were tortured. Rebellion spread though the camp.

Some escaped and turned toward home. A few plotted to wait and turn on their captors in the midst of battle. Scouts were dispatched. Screams startled men in the night. No one reported back.

Bodies of the scouts were found hanging from a tree. Reluctant men slipped into the forest in search of their tormentors. They did not return.

Some warriors of the NorBlad took heart that the gods did not favor the unspoken ways after all. They had yet to see the powerful magic that the voices of the unspoken claimed to have. Perhaps this was the sign to redeem themselves and die as warriors. Their women and children would die in the mounds, but meet them again in Tor's halls. The horrible manner of their deaths would be forgotten amid the protection of the fierce god's maiden wives.

Determined not to fail Ottfried, the commander moved down the mountain. The following days were marked by forced marches and nights of demons screaming in the dark. Another night of missing guards, morning light revealing swollen corpses twisted in death agony, vicious wounds on neck and chest.

Seven days later nearly one quarter of the rabble were dead or deserters. The bandits were terrified, the NorBlad sullen and plotting. Eskil's men were wary and herding an untrustworthy lot to fight. Never said aloud was the fear the unspoken had abandoned them.

Raven rode ahead of the enemy. He wondered if Ullric was returning with Jerred's army. He was tired and needed to report what he knew. Chi increased his pace as the terrain became less treacherous. He did not slow during the night and Raven did not give thought to the animal's ability to traverse the hills in some times total darkness. He slept. Much later they passed a troop of horsemen. His spirits lifted, they were Jerred's men. None of the guards detected their passage.

Jerred's forces had not moved as fast as hoped. They were not at Rayna Pass when Ullric got there and it took another day to find them. His news was incentive to greater effort. Jerred planned to ambush the rabble army when they reached easier terrain. To that end the majority of wagons and supplies were left behind to arrive at their own pace. Ullric made sure his pack was outfitted and snatched Raven's war bag.

He led a group of archers to position themselves along the only viable trail. He directed mounted warriors to ride swiftly west and double back to attack from the rear. Once this rabble was defeated, Jerred would leave part of his forces to hold the pass over the mountains and keep the reserve supplies. He had been promised continuous delivery of arms and food.

Jerred needed a victory if he would keep these homesteaders and noble's sons in the field.

A look out warned Ullric of a rider's approach but was unable to determine whether friend or foe. Chi galloped into view and halted directly before Ullric's hiding place. The big blonde stepped from cover, scowling and disturbed. Every time he thought he could deal with the animal, it did something else unsettling.

Chi was lathered. They had traveled hard and knowing them, though the night.

"They are a day, maybe two behind me. The leaders are no longer sure of themselves. Nearly thirty are dead or deserted."

Ullric's gaped at the man.

"What did you...?"

"Frightened them. They turned on each other. Some of your people escaped and headed north again. Some..."

"The devils take them. The damned cowards, I..."

"Give over Ullric! Hear me. I think others plan to strike down Ottfried's men as soon as a battle is joined. Dedric has consigned all able-bodied men and boys for the raids. He has taken many prisoners, women and babes. Men were told if they did not fight their families would be sacrificed. Give them a chance, they are your people."

Ullric snarled. "The devil's take them. If they had forced Dedric out when he first started this madness none of us would be here. These rabble have no magic. They are mad men who prey on fears."

"You said your packs are feared by all. Let them turn their hatred to Dedric and Ottfried. We could strike in many places with your people guiding us."

One of the Lua second stepped from the bush.

"He speaks sense big one. If they turn on their captors it will be easy enough to spare them. If not my sisters can eliminate them or the mounted ones waiting to trap them up there. Either way we will not loose this battle."

"I have much to hate them for, but you make sense. So be it. We will do as planned. But I will spare none if they continue to fawn over their captors."

With that he stomped off to fume in private.

"Come Thanatu, I will show you where we camp."

Chi followed her deep into the dense vegetation. Other archers were resting there, eating or sleeping. The glade was silent except for the distant sound of flowing water. Raven dismounted and relieved Chi of saddle and bridle. The horse moved away before he could be rubbed down. Raven put his gear beneath a thick pine, stretched out on the ground and was instantly asleep.

Near dark, Ullric returned to the camp. He sat and stared at the dark haired warrior sleeping beneath the trees. Could he believe the man? Thirty men? He could well imagine Raven killing many in the dark. Had he not come close to being one of the dead? He had seen dark deeds written in the young man's eyes. He remembered the disbelief in his hoarse voice when he discovered what a sacrifice to the unspoken ones meant. Ullric wondered what revenge Raven claimed for his outrage. Then he wondered if he really wanted to know.

Before the sun crested the mountains, twenty-five Lua had taken position in the valley through which the invaders must pass. Other routes lead to unpopulated areas with more treacherous terrain. The commander was committed to this course. Retribution must be administered to all non- believers.

Ullric considered all westerners must train in 'hiding to kill a man'.

He could not see the Lua once they settled in their places. A man should face his enemy and die with a sword in his hand. But then again, the filth from the ice caps were not men. They deserved a shameful death and exclusion from Tor's halls.

Raven slept deeply, as still as a corpse. Chi appeared occasionally to nuzzle him and then vanish. Ullric would have checked on him, but the memory of hissing snakes in the dark kept him rooted to his little patch of ground. The Lua paid neither of them any mind at all.

Scouts for the mounted troops reported the raider's passing by. The company moved out trailing behind the rabble, their horse's hooves muffled with rags. Hours later scouts reported a few bandits attempting to leave were beheaded. The indentured NorBlad were not armed and the bandits wanted to abandon the unspoken. The horsemen waited impatiently. The Lua had first strike. Even with their numbers a bunch of fanatics would make a hard fight of it.

The bolts of the Lua longbows struck like lightening. Men were transfixed to the ground, some attempting to pull their bodies off the metal tipped shafts when the second wave struck. Eskil screamed defiance and ordered his men to attack. They scrambled for cover when another fall of bolts continued to deplete their forces. NorBlad turned on their captors with bare hands and killed them with their own weapons. Others armed themselves from the wagons.

Shrieks of berserker rage rang through the column. Ullric sent warning for everyone to beware. A berserk NorBlad recognized neither friend nor foe. Jerred's mounted forces hit the rear of the unspoken screaming for revenge. The clash of steel echoed for miles.

Ullric entered the fight, the remnants of the Wolf pack at his back. His battle-axe smashed skulls and hacked men in two. Noak, Ivo and Elika roared their challenges and beat the enemy into the earth with axe and hammer. Unlike the past, Ullric did not give in to the blood lust of battle. Now responsible for a field of lowlanders who did not trust him the NorBlad had to keep his head and not turn on them himself. He ignored the screams of fear and the cries of the dying. Lua remained out of sight, their arrows falling less often but with lethal accuracy. A NorBlad attacked him. Ullric cut him down and met the next opponent.

The bandits were totally immobilized. They had expected easy prey like always, striking this new deal in happy anticipation of greater booty. They had been set upon by their allies, attacked in the night by devils and now faced an army of mercenaries and farmers! Many attempted to flee; both sides of the conflict butchered them to a man.

Raven and Chi entered the fight. Hair stood up all over Ullric's body as that horrible hiss reached his ears. He turned to strike at the demon, only to find him yards away. Raven's sword cut through the swarming mass like a scythe through plains grass. Some men did not fall until he moved to the next, their faces shocked when limbs fell from them before dying. His actions were swift and silent under the sun as in the dark. The main body of horsemen was still some distance away.

Many, thinking to bring this new swordsman down, converged on the duo, only to have their throats ripped out by the horse. Then Chi screamed and Ullric heard what had terrorized men in the night. Chi struck again, flinging his captive away and striking another as fast as a snake. The blade flashed in the sun. Blood splashed against the animal's hide. Raven's face was red with the blood of his opponents. It floated on the air around the duo like fog. Soon the area around him was clear of foes and he moved once again into the thick of it.

Rage ate at Ullric, he ached to give into it. But Dedric still remained and he must wait. They fought until no one had the strength to continue. A few of the NorBlad died gripped by shame and berserk rage. They were felled by terrified fighters on both sides. The unspoken followers fought to the last, their bodies mutilated long after death had claimed them. Raven did not stop until the field was silent. He fully embraced the beliefs of the Thanatu. Severely wounded should not be left to suffer and a brave fighter should not be tortured for information he surely would not have. No one stopped him. Ullric was busy rounding up the surviving NorBlad.

Eskil was, unfortunately for him, taken alive. He was dragged from the brush by Lua and turned over to Ullric. The warrior spat on the trembling man. Many had died while he sought cover. His defiance now was laughable. The sword was still in his scabbard. Eskil would know Ottfried's plans. With a jerk of his head, Ullric consigned him to the wolf pack. Ivo and Noak dragged him away. Elika was in the hands of the Lua having a minor wound stitched up. They insisted and the big man could not refuse the little women.

The red head watched the prisoner's passage so he could join them later. He was still aroused, the smell of blood and fear thick in his nostrils. Between the three of them the scum would tell all he knew.

Ullric called his captains together. The mounted force was to be commended. Although many were untried, they fought hard. As Jerred advised him, Ullric went to see the wounded and helped build the pyres for the dead. The young man told him an expression of concern would insure the people would come to trust him.

It was not the NorBlad way. A warrior fought, if he could not leave the field he ended his own life or bled to death. If he could walk back home, his family took care of his healing. Pyres were reserved for the bravest of pack warriors. Jerred's people spent much time consoling the wounded and grieving. He marveled that many men and women who fought so viciously, now cried and wailed. He took no part in this. Not even the women of his tribe grieved in public. He returned to his camp and searched for his men.

Screams lead him to Elika bent over and gasping for breath. Eskil's battered body was on the ground and his wailing never stopped.

"Hold pack brother. I would have him with voice enough to answer my questions."

Elika looked up. His face was twisted and ugly with contempt towards the coward lying at this feet.

Ivo answered for him. His curly white blonde hair was still black with the blood of his enemies.

"He just screams like a woman. This whimpering

fool will tell us nothing."

Ullric laughed and raised Eskil's head.

"Look at me filth. Perhaps my brother's are too gentle for you?"

The three men growled and Elika kicked the man against a fallen pine. Eskil bit through his lip as skin was scrapped from his groin and belly. He was smeared with the sweat and blood from the dead that covered the bodies of his tormentors.

"If you do not tell me what Ottfried has planned I will break you one bone at a time, all night if needs be. I will stake you by my fires to be my dog. Even a cripple cur will howl to save his hide from a good beating."

Ullric spat when he said it, face grotesque with hatred.

Eskil moaned, his head held up by the hair in Elika's big fist. The NorBlad before him looked bigger than the men who had beaten him already. He knew now that death, which he decreed for others without hesitation, would have been preferable to this endless torture. He begged then, for the torture to end, for a quick death. The unspoken had abandoned Ottfried and they were all doomed. Ullric laughed.

"You hid in the bush. Even your followers fought like warriors until we killed them. The death of a warrior is not for the likes of you. I will keep you on a lead and you will follow at my heels like a good hound.

I will allow my pack to use you whenever they wish. We have no women. You filth have killed them all! But a man must have release after a battle. Maybe we will make due, though you have nothing about you to appeal to a warrior." He laughed then, a nasty bitter cackle edged with madness.

Eskil continued to cry and beg. Ullric slapped him, then yanked the forward by the neck and strangled him. Eskil tried desperately to draw air into his lungs. He wet himself, again. The former celebrant of the unspoken thrashed around on the log until he lost consciousness, and Ullric waited...

Raven had ridden far from the battle site. He did not want to hear the sounds of the captive being tortured for information. The NorBlad had their ways. But torture always made Raven ill and despairing. He remembered the warriors in the mound and the past that haunted his dreams.

He dismounted and washed in the icy water. When he was clean and dressed in dry clothes, Raven bent to the task of cleaning his bloody leathers. Chi lolled in the water for a while, then found a place for Raven to rest. The big not horse settled near him, lending his body heat while his charge slept.

Jerred sat easy in the saddle. When the column crested another peak, he looked back at the NorBlad survivors loaded down with his army's supplies. The scattered snow made the way treacherous. The wagons had to be left behind and Ullric declared the survivors of their first battle were the only way to get the cargo over the mountain. Not one voiced a protest.

The NorBlad were shocked to see him alive and shamed beyond facing him. Some of them had literally slammed doors in his face when he fled through the night trying to protect his elders and a few surviving women. He vowed on Tor's name that if one faltered from this moment he would be tortured to death and left for the carrion eaters. Eskil survived, black with bruises and blood, tethered to a stake in the ground at night near Ivo's tent. He was fed scraps and watered like a dog. Whenever Ullric came near he would whimper and grovel.

In this Jerred did not interfere though it disgusted him. Ullric would keep the filth alive enough to wring more information out of him. To spare himself anymore of their attention, Eskil babbled readily when questioned.

Jerred had seen the aftermath of the fight. He heard the accounts of events from nearly everyone. His people spoke of Raven in awed whispers, silent welder of death and Chi, a screaming fiend of slashing fangs and odd snake like movements. Neither had been seen since the battle ended. The Lua assured Jerred the Thanatu was nearby. He never abandoned a contract.

After they left the horses it took two weeks to cross the mountain range and camp along the cliffs of the pass. The rocky landscape provided what they needed to build fortifications and shelter them from howling winds and snow. After much discussion, it was decided when the storm passed each of Ullric's pack brothers would take a small scouting party to discover what movement, if any, Dedric and Ottfried had made.

It was an unpleasant surprise not to find any fighters massing for an attack. Could Dedric be attacking on another front after all? He would loose more men than not any other way. Ullric wondered if the two madmen had turned on each other. There may be nothing for Jerred's army to do but go home.

Ullric stood on a ledge. An over hang protected him from the worst of the wind.

"Ullric..."

He spun, axe swinging, to find Raven perched on a boulder a foot away.

"Devils taken you Thanatu! You know better than to sneak up on a man! Where have you been? Jerred thinks you abandoned us."

"You wanted us to find out what Dedric's plans were. So we did."

"How could you? You have never been here. How would you know?"

"I talked to your countrymen before we left. We were careful."

Ullric took a long look at the warrior. Raven's face was shadowed by beard, his hair unbound and shaggy. He wore a coat made from snow bear fur over gray tunic and breeches. His eyes were red and his face pale.

"Come, I will take you to Jerred's fire. You look like hot food would be welcome."

Raven grunted and turned away, climbing down the side of the cliff where Chi waited. Ullric followed and then led them to a depression in the mountainside where Jerred had set up a headquarters. Raven sighed with relief when they stepped into the cave. He was cold, tired and very dirty.

"Jerred, Raven is back."

The young lord came to his feet immediately and rushed to greet them.

"Thank the gods. I thought you left us."

"You pay gold. I stay until the end."

"Forgive me. I mean no offense. I was worried."

Raven looked the younger man in the eye assessing, then nodded.

"I knew you needed information. We rode ahead. I have to tell you..."

"Can it wait until you are rested? You look near collapse."

The dark warrior rubbed grimy hands over his face.

"There is time. We could sleep."

"Come and eat first." Ullric jerked his head toward the fire. He went and knelt down, filling a wooden bowl with hot stew. He tore a chunk of coarse bread off a big loaf and dropped it in the bowl. Raven shook off his coat and seeing an unoccupied corner, dropped his travel bag and removed Chi's saddle.

There were several other men by the fire. Noak for one, mercenary captains and those aligned with noble houses. They watched warily as he approached and took the bowl from Ullric. Firelight glinted off Thanatu blades worn at his back.

"Thank you... I could eat a horse."

Chi snorted. For a moment there was silence and then Ullric laughed. He surprised himself, the joke was between this man and his, whatever Chi was. Raven smiled, more with his eyes than his grim mouth, then shuffled back to the corner. He hunkered down and ate with the single-minded devotion of the near starving. Ullric frowned.

When he finished, Ullric took the bowl and filled it again under Chi's watchful eyes. Raven did everything but lick it clean.

"When did you eat last?"

"There was a mountain goat some time back. But I let Chi have most of it. When I left the battlefield I could not eat for many days. It is always like that."

"There should have been ox for you to hunt. Good meat, fat."

"Saw sign of some kind of herd animals, but they had moved out of range. I needed to find our quarry."

He sat the bowl down and drank from his water skin, then yawned so wide his jaw popped. He pulled the blanket from his bag and wrapped himself tightly.

"You could get closer to the fire." Jerred offered.

"Thank you, but I will be all right here." Raven's voice was raspy with fatigue and the hot food in his belly was rapidly pulling him down.

Jerred made some small move that Ullric aborted with a big hand on his chest.

"Leave it. When he is down the demon is most dangerous."

They all looked up as Raven lay down on his coat. Chi nuzzled his body and turned his soft gaze on the men at the fire. Ullric could not seem to control his response.

"None of us are so foolish to bother him after seeing you fight."

His companions looked at him in surprise.

"We will stay away."

Chi snorted and lowered his body to the ground in front of Raven and was asleep in seconds.

Jerred was looking at him with wide questioning gaze.

"You should tell your people if the Thanatu is wounded or down for any reason, leave him. Chi will kill anyone who tries to aid him. He does not seem to care if you are friend or foe."

"At least he seemed to know during the battle. He plucked a berserk NorBlad off of me like the man was a feather. He shook him like a hound with a rabbit and tossed him away." The man shuddered at the memory, grateful to be alive to fight another day, but frightened by what he saw. No horse could rake away a man's face with great fangs like a serpent.

"He seems to know a lot of things. I would give a year."

"Hold there. Do not dare whatever you are thinking. You may find more than you want to and die in the attempt."

"The Lua say the horses are sometimes seen in their country. They have nothing fast enough to catch them. They only go to Thanatu."

"I want to know why Dedric has no raiding parties in the pass. Why we have not been attacked."

"If the word was urgent he would have said so. Perhaps there is strife between these allies. Maybe they are now fighting among themselves."

"It would shorten our stay here. I would leave you NorBlad to decide Dedric's fate, once we have him. But Ottfried must be killed at all costs. We dare not leave him to prey on people again. I would not want that stench to cause trouble another day because we did not go to the ice walls themselves to find him."

The men about the fire stirred uneasily, but they knew the young lord was right. Dedric had not lead a raid for many seasons and was probably insane, but a tribe of fanatical warriors protected Ottfried. Truly that is where the fighting would be.

"Humph. Enough talk. We should all sleep now."

There were grunts of agreement. After some shuffling around and last comments the men and women wrapped in their blankets. Ullric stretched out before Jerred and Noak lay near him. He dared to trust only his pack mates with the young lord's safety. If anything happened to Jerred his people would turn on them all. This alliance was not sound. You cannot end centuries of warfare overnight and expect trust to replace suspicion and hatred.

Contrary to belief, there was little gold in his land. The raids below storms had provided goods and women more often than gold. The silver the NorBlad scraped together would be nothing to tempt the mercenary companies to remain. He did not know what the Thanatu would do, but it was a given that the Lua would remain to fulfill their contract, even if the young lord died. The women had already fortified their positions in the pass. No one would get through it alive with fifty Lua and their repeating crossbows, less there be a blizzard. Their presence may keep the other lord's men here, at least for a while. The pass could be held against the NorBlad easily.

Ullric realized, had Rykk and the ones before him not been frightened cattle, the NorBlad would have been contained long ago. Otto was right. To trade with these people was the only way to insure the continued existence of his tribe. Pain knotted in his chest. His people? Otto and Grete were dead. The women and children that were part of Otto's household were dead. Grete had yet to conceive and Ullric was grateful. Dedric would have probably consigned the child to the mounds, terrorizing it to death.

For the first time he wondered what he would do if he survived the fight. His pack mates had blood in other packs and should be able to start again. All that he loved were dead and the sight of his people sickened him. In his dreams death birds suppered on the dead while their namesake slept a few feet from him.

Chi was not asleep. His lay surrounded by lesser ones. Even in sleep their nervousness permeated the cave.

Men feared all things, even that which did not exist. He snorted, the big one shifted and looked into his eyes. Whatever he saw made him twist his face in a knot and turn over. Chi snorted, more than once, just to watch the shoulders twitch. This one amused him, angry with himself because Chi frightened him. He should be frightened. It must always be so.

Snow fell during the night. Fires were rekindled and porridge cooked to ward off the damp. Men and women huddled together cursed the NorBlad and the land that produced them. The storm did not wan during the day.

Raven was as dead. Ullric wondered how far they went before turning back. Weather did not deter NorBlad. There should be men here slavering for blood, but the land was stark and silent. He finally moved closer to the fire. Jerred's men drank a black tea they favored. He drank it as a courtesy. A tankard of good strong ale would have served better, but Jerred had forbid strong spirits. He did not turn away from the stew bubbling over the fire either. Periodically someone would glance at the duo resting in the corner but refrained from speaking.

Chi swung his dark head toward the fire sometime during the night. Raven came to his feet and stepped into the storm. After a moment he returned, dried the wet from his body and hair with the bear coat, and settled at the fire. He accepted hot tea and food from Ullric. No one spoke until he was eating his third bowl.

"Enough of this silence. What news have you? Speak man, speak!" One of the mercenary captains urged him, finally irritated beyond bearing with the silence. Raven turned his silver gaze to Ullric and Jerred.

"Ottfried sits in the hall of your chieftain. Dedric's body is pinned to the door with an axe."

Shocked silence once again allowed the wind to howl outside the cave like a lost soul.

"His men are gathering to raid below storms. They do not rush. The NorBlad do not come with him. Many died in a battle and their bodies lie frozen on the plains. The survivors have fled the villages. I could find them, but would they listen to a stranger? I think there are enough left to continue the fight, but no one is strong enough to bring them together. A few have already killed each other over who will lead."

Ullric and Noak jumped to their feet and howled in murderous rage. Jerred's men sprang away from the fire in surprise, reaching for their weapons. Raven continued to sit by the fire and finished his meal. Ullric ran into the storm with Noak on his heels. The others shifted nervously. Would Ullric turn on them and have to be killed? Jerred was shocked by their reaction to Raven's news.

"Do not go after them. Come back to the fire. There is one you cannot save. His life is not worth your men dying for."

It took a moment for his words to sink in. A shriek

let them know Ullric found a target for his rage.

"Eskil, they went after Eskil." Jerred whispered then dropped to the ground, not caring if the men saw his fear.

More than one trembling set of hands reached for warmth. Ullric was so big and so much stronger, no one wished to face him and certainly not berserk.

"Raven, is it possible to gather the NorBlad to fight again?"

"If Ullric goes among them with some of the survivors of our battle, I think he could rally them. Right now they don't have one man strong enough to lead them. From what I understand the packs unite on occasion for mutual gain, so even though this is survival, many will not let go of past hatreds."

One of the captains spat in the fire. He was seeing the ferocious NorBlad fight for the first time.

"No one would believe we fight to save NorBlad. Our children's children will say we are mad to tell such tales."

"We could be fending off NorBlad in hopeless skirmishes now if not for Dedric's treachery. No one of us would be here fighting if the lowland nobles did not think themselves threatened." Jerred sipped at the tea, wishing for a tankard of brandy from his cellar.

"Well, my lord thought you stretched the truth about the danger to get his help. Perhaps the gods guided you boy, for this has been more than we would have dreamed."

Jerred only nodded at the comment, his thoughts out in the storm wondering if Ullric would return in right mind to finish this fight.

"My lord, my lord. You must come! The NorBlad, they--" The guardsman stumbled and fell in the entrance, unable to speak further in his panic.

Jerred grabbed his coat and rushed from the cave. His captains followed, weapons ready. Raven scowled at their backs, annoyed at the thought of going out in the storm.

In the driving snow and howling winds NorBlad were gathering. Ullric's pack mates were handing out weapons. Jerred rushed to Ullric's side.

"What do you Ullric? You cannot fight Ottfried by yourselves!" He had to shout into the wind not sure if Ullric heard him. The big warrior's hands were blood drenched and Jerred recoiled.

"I go boy. I go and destroy the cowards who have brought us to this. I go to avenge my brother's death. They will fight or they will die and the NorBlad will be no more." His face was twisted with rage. He turned away for Jerred. When the young man attempted to stop him, many hands held him back. Ullric howled into the wind. His pack mates joined him. A shout went up and all the surviving northern warriors threw themselves into the storm. Jerred was dismayed. Ullric would not reason now. What should he do?

Though many of his fighters sprang from the same stock, they were not use to conditions such as these to fight in. He hoped to catch Ottfried's men in the pass where the Lua would cut their numbers. Then his warriors would fall upon the survivors and eliminate the threat of Ottfried. Damned the NorBlad blood lust!

"Captains, go to your troops. Tell them all is well. Ullric will fight, but most of Ottfried's men will march on the pass. We will have our chance, but it will not come soon. We must wait for now. Check your supplies and report to me soon as you can."

The fighters rushed off, anxious to get out of the weather and reassure their people. Jerred turned back to his shelter, relieved to find Raven still there.

"I want you to go after him."

"It will have the same results in the end. Ullric may be distraction, but most of Ottfried's will come for the pass. We will wait for this storm to pass. I do not like snow. If Ullric can be convinced, a direct attack on this creature while his men are here fighting you could end this. I never saw him, but I do not think he plans to lead his men in this."

"Ullric may be past reason now. What then?"

"Then after fighting here you must cross into the NorBlad lands to fight before true winter comes."

"Fighting through the winter has never been an option for us. This land barely supports the NorBlad this time of year. My people would not fair well."

"Another hundred gold coins and I will kill Ottfried for you. Even if we leave and I must return in the summer."

"I will consider it. The way things are going now, it may be my only option."

Jerred sat back by the fire, dejected at the turn of events. If Ullric's mad dash did not exhaust his rage, he would not listen to Raven. He would not extol his people to fight the unspoken ones, he would kill them himself. If he did agree to the Thanatu's plan, Ottfried's threat could be eliminated forever. Too many ifs. He watched Raven settle down and begin a through job of cleaning his blades. The young man wished he had the self-assurance that Raven seemed to possess. He handled whatever came to him and worried not at all about the rest.

Two days later the storm ended. The sun did not break through the heavy clouds, but did lend a bit of twilight to the mountain pass. Raven rode away, Jerred watching him cross the white plain from the cliff side where Ullric had stood a few days before. He did not come down until Chi's dark hide could no longer be seen.

Chi settled into a ground-consuming gallop, the

wind carrying the scent of NorBlad to him. They were not too far ahead even with rage fueling their passage. Raven slipped into the link with his companion where the cold and damp air did not taunt him. He would be a long time returning to the land below storms to work. The weather there was annoying but this icy waste was unbearable. As soon as this ended he would travel south to the barrens and maybe beyond since he had never ventured there.

Ullric moved swiftly, the warriors on his heels. They had barely stopped to rest, fighting the weather with the same stubbornness as they did an enemy. His world was sundered and Ullric would have blood for it. Any in his path that did not join would die. Occasionally he howled his anguish, the pack taking it up, the others howling and growling the war cries of their broken clans. They ran on.

The gray dawn of another morning was rapidly lowering to more storm clouds when one of the men rushed to his side, pointing to the southwest. Even at a distance Ullric knew it was Raven. Jerred would not send any of his own people to dare the icy waste in such weather. Too many-feared Ullric to dare stop him. He was furious and ran to confront the Thanatu who moved to meet him on foot.

"I will not be turned you Thanatu whelp. I back down to no man, demon or not!" His axe whistled in the wind.

Raven was not intimidated.

"I have not come to stop you Ullric. I have come to ride with you."

His voice was soft, barely heard above the wind.

Taken off guard, Ullric lowered his axe and stared.

"Why? Jerred tried to stop us."

"We think if your people will gather around you, Ottfried's hall could be attacked while his men move on the pass. I do not think Ottfried intends to go with his men. You NorBlad could have your revenge. With out the head, the body of the serpent should be easy to kill. Move from the path you take so the unspoken ones to not see you."

"And if you are wrong?"

"Then great fool, you come behind them and attack from the rear. Ottfried would be trapped and eventually die in the pass by Jerred's troop or your own clans."

Ullric bristled at the words, but held himself. Jerred always thought things through and listened to council. The NorBlad always fought first and talked of their battles over the spoils. You fight and won, or died. Jerred was here when the entire history of both peoples would have denied such a thing. And Ottfried, a serpent at their backs, nearly eliminated his people without risking anything. A great sigh welled up from his chest, sounding like a moan of pain when released.

"In this I will be guided Thanatu. I will go as you say." His great shoulders slumped and for a moment his pain showed through the facade of rage.

"I promise you this NorBlad. Your axe will feast on the blood of your enemies."

They turned back to Ullric's men, Raven keeping pace as the group trotted off into the darkening day. Chi did not join them and Ullric did not think to ask after it.

Ullric's pack mates and a few others carefully chosen, had gone ahead to the cliffs where the survivors would hide. There were also a few clans Ottfried had left unmolested. It was nearly three weeks since the revelation of Dedric's shameful death. Many of these had not known until Ullric's men arrived at their villages. Now they sat around a dead campfire far from home and ill at ease. Many of the faces were drawn with fatigue and sickness.

"Why should we trust you Ullric? Before your pack spoke of trade and peace," he spat in the snow, "we feared nothing. Ottfried would not be here..."

Shouts of support and outrage went up from the group. Ullric sprang to his feet and bellowed.

"With your body, you lover of mounds! No one raised arms against Dedric. He struck down his most loyal and dragged our women and children to the sacrifice with his own hands! Ottfried made use of his madness and no one NorBlad raised hands to defy him."

"You know Ottfried talks to demons. You know they have great mag..."

"Magic be damned!" Ullric roared. "There is no such thing you addled..."

"You run and come back with our enemies and say they will fight with us. Do you put this Jerred in our halls to lord over us?"

The urge to kill moved strong in him. Ullric laughed long and hard, nearly unable to stop.

"Jerred wants no part of us. For the first time in memory the name of our people inspires laughter. How many are dead in the mounds? How many died on the plain when they finally choked on their cowardice and fought. We are walking dead. Our women and children have been abandoned to rape and sacrifice because you fear magic. There are none of us left to make raids on the land below storms. Jerred would stop Ottfried from spreading his filth to the lowlands. If Jerred is successful the lords there will rise up, to keep us from raiding ever again. Hold your contempt fool."

He turned on a jeering older man, his hair streaked with white.

"Jerred is a warrior, not a spineless wyrm like those that ruled before him. Fighters have come from all over for this fight. Many brave the winter here for gold, but more to protect their homes. If you let this scum hold our lands, you will have fighters here like you have never seen. Lua have come and Thanatu. These have only been legend to us, but I have seen them fight.

We have the weapons we hold and the weather. That is not enough to stop Ottfried or Jerred from letting the winter work it's ill and then sweep over us like a plague. With the other lords backing, Jerred can eventually destroy Ottfried without us. Coward and NorBlad will be one word."

He spit in the fire. Acid roiled in his stomach. How could he be here begging NorBlad to fight? Some place inside of him twisted and withered.

For moments after he spoke the men were silent. Some of these clans had stood fast to Dedric and now found Ottfried making noise about bringing them to the sacrifice. When the other clans decided to fight instead of remaining cattle for Ottfried's sacrifices, these men or their leaders had seen no point and turned away or took their survivors deep in the wastelands to start again.

Of the latter, few found welcome among their fellows. Some were put to the sword in hopes Ottfried would be pleased. Ottfried had not even bothered to send his warriors after them. The land rang with the taunts of his followers, extolling these NorBlad to give them selves up. Was it not better to die in the mounds for the glory of unspoken, than die running like curs, with tails tucked between their legs?

Always before the clans stood alone, except during the season of raiding. Dedric was the first among them to call himself king and hold them to a loose alliance. Look where it got them. Now Ullric wanted them to follow him with more of their enemies at his back.

One of them stood and faced Ullric.

"I am Tait. Twelve are all that is left of Ox. We will go with you Ullric and fight with your Wolf pack.

I will take the blood of my enemies to Tor's halls."

"May I drink with you there, Tait of the Ox."

The young man nodded and left the circle. His father had come here over the protest of the young survivors. The clans did not welcome them. All his life he was taught to obey the elders, but his continued protest finally lead to confrontation and the old warrior forced Tait to fight. The boy's heart ached to think that he would not find his father drinking at the table with Tor's wives. Here they were shunned and scraped for survival. What honor was in this life when their fellows died fighting Ottfried on the plains and his people hid? He went quickly to tell his friends and move to Ullric's camp.

"We will follow you Ullric. I am Gus, chosen by the Fox pack to speak for them. All our elders supported Dedric, even when Ottfried dragged off my mother and sisters. We are not blooded in battle and the oldest has never even raided, but we would go Ullric, we would go."

Ullric looked on the pale face of a mere stripling. He was tall but still lacking the bulk of adulthood, no more than twelve or thirteen seasons. His face was gaunt, shadowed with hunger. No one of the others had raised hand to feed these children. Only the strong survived. It was ever the way of NorBlad.

"Go and gather your pack. We will share what stores we have until you enter Tor's halls. There is no hunger there."

The boy flung himself onto Ullric's great chest and hugged him tight, then ran into the trees. Would Ullric find that there were only children left with the will to fight?

"So you will take children and fight Ottfried," derisive laughter scattered around the circle.

"Better that than hiding behind rocks and pissing my legs in fear."

The warrior drew his sword and Ullric leaped to meet him. Steel struck and slide along the axe blade, sparks flew. Ullric beat the other fighter back. He did not stop until the man's head was obliterated in the snow. He turned to ward off another blow and gave in to berserk rage so long contained.

Most of the warriors leapt from his path. Six men made to fight him. His axe bite deep and stuck in the chest of his next assailant. Ullric planted his feet and wrenched at the blade, then kicked another in the chest swinging the body on the end of his axe in the path of the others. The body fell away, the back blade catching another man in the head. Steel rang together and men shouted epitaphs depending where their tenuous support lay. The axe swung and reversed in air that moaned through its passing. A skull cracked, an arm fell still clutching its sword. The body of the fallen warrior tripped one of his companions. The axe clove that one's skull in two. Without hesitation Ullric smashed in the skull of the one armed warrior trying to drag his body from the fight.

Bellowing his challenge, the blond giant threw himself on the remaining men. They fought because no choice remained. The smart ones had fled. Somehow they must make peace with Ullric and fight Ottfried, if they survived this night.

When awareness returned, the meeting place was strewn with carrion. Ullric was on his knees, lungs straining for air after his exertions. Eventually he staggered away. He returned to the main camp by instinct alone, going to his rough fur without a word to anyone. His men kept their eyes averted. The sounds of battle and dying men had reached their ears quite clearly.

One could easily provoke a warrior after a berserk

rage. Even his pack mates stayed clear.

During the following days fighters arrived, mostly the ravaged clans of the plains. Envoys from the cliff dwelling clans brought rations and their fighters. Ullric sat glaring at everyone, his mind and body mired in blood. He did not speak and everyone avoided him. Raven was a shadow that many newcomers did not believe existed.

When Ullric finally stood and threw off his fur, the broken clans gathered around him. His green eyes glittered with hatred.

"The first to hesitate dies. Some sent warning to Ottfried, your messengers are dead. I will kill his men and I will kill any of you that will not fight. I will return here and make sure that the blood of cowards never flows in the veins of NorBlad again. If you would not raise a hand to fight for your own, you certainly will not stop me from killing all of you. Go now and know I will snap at your heels like a starving bear every step of the way."

The NorBlad ran before him, the suspect clans surrounded by the few Ullric trusted. Chi and Raven haunted the dark. In the morning bodies were discovered decapitated or ripped apart. Ullric laughed and gibbered in conversations with himself. But let one attempt to fall behind and he would be quick as a serpent to strike.

So it was the NorBlad crept upon Ottfried's hall with unusual stealth.

Few men patrolled the sparse trees and Raven discovered the hall was not heavily manned. Snow churned to mud and refrozen marked the path of a large group of men headed toward the pass where Jerred waited for news.

The ones left behind drank with abandon and jeered the whimpering victims imprisoned in a mound before the decrepit hall. Raven thought it might be possible to save some of the women and children whose smothered cries seem to find him even in the depths of the boulder strewn forest.

The fighters obeyed orders that to them made little sense. They hid themselves in snow and struck from ambush to take down the guards. They fired the walls surrounding the hall just before dawn and with a raving Ullric at their backs, attacked.

Ottfried burst from the doors where Dedric's frozen corpse still hung. The unspoken leader was covered in wild brown hair, knotted with the finger bones of women and children. The skull of a baby hung from his neck and offal smeared his body and filthy furs. He fought with club and hammer smashing his opponents, and foaming at the mouth. The unspoken followers screamed the while, cursed their attackers and fought like ten devils. Ullric erupted in the midst of them, his axe severing heads and cleaving spines.

A bloodcurdling scream heralded the Thanatu's entry into battle. His blades rose and fell, showers of blood falling like banners on the frosted earth. Chi snatched many and snapped their necks. How he knew friend from foe would forever remain a mystery. The yard was packed with fighting men, the hall and out buildings ablaze. Smoke obscured vision and stole precious breath. Men fought with bare hands, gouging and tearing flesh in desperation.

Wind brought a sudden shower of stinging sleet and snow as the day wore on. Ullric had hurled himself at Ottfried, only to be forced back as many times by the filth's loyal followers. But now, his men had whittled them down. Raven slipped beneath the guard of sword and axe welders striking with both blades and moving on. He cleared a path to Ottfried that Ullric was quick to step into.

Disregarding dozens of minor wounds and creeping fatigue, the NorBlad confronted the usurper of his world. There was no breath left for chest beating, only to lift their weapons with trembling limbs and fight.

Raven wove a circle of death around the combatants. None could see clearly in the swirling snow and smoke. True dark's arrival further obscured the site. Finally the survivors could only hear the continued clash of arms. Anyone approaching was met with stinging sword point or death. Long after the last of Ottfried's men died, the battle between him and Ullric raged on.

Suddenly a heavy silence fell upon the yard. Weapons were once again posed to strike. From the smoking ruins stepped Ullric, Ottfried's head on a broken sword blade, gore running over his hand. He tossed it at the feet of the surviving warriors.

"Here is that which you fear great NorBlad," he rasped, "a man like any other. One who dies like any other."

And he spat upon the snow and dragged his weary body away. His hoarse voice floated back to them.

"You are not done yet--mighty--fighters. There are others yet to kill, if Jerred has not done it for you."

Raven snared the fighters suffering the least wounds and set them to digging out the mound. The Thanatu worried, for no cries encouraged the men the closer they got to breaking through the ice packed mud walls. The stench of rotting flesh staggered everyone, then Raven crawled inside and dragged two weeping women from the hole. One clutched a dead child to her breast and the other lay staring, not responding even when they attempted to quench her obvious thirst and hunger. She died in Raven's arms and the other woman impaled herself on a shattered blade rather than abandon her babe.

So they left the ruins and sheltered amid the scorched trees and boulders. When he awakened, Ullric built a pyre and searched the carnage for the bodies of Ox and Fox. He gathered all the remains he could and lit the fire. He and his wolf brothers began the death song.

He forced the others to sing, all of them must raise their voices. The children were escorted to Tor's halls with honor reserved for their greatest clan leaders. Then Ullric decreed that no one would claim the name of Ox and Fox ever again. None were entitled.

Scouts sent out after Raven's departure returned to the pass. Ottfried's men were on the move. The weather assisted in eliminating signs of Jerred's army. They were dug in well and the timely arrival of additional supplies had boosted moral even more. Now the foul creatures were coming and the fight would soon be joined. There had been no word of Ullric and Raven, but contrary to his captains concerns, Jerred kept faith all would be well.

Raven and his strange mount had proven themselves to his complete satisfaction. They were his miracles and he would not entertain ill words about them. He hoped in his heart that Ullric would see reason. The man had proved a canny and reasonable leader, contrary to first impressions, but the berserk was a thing beyond his control. Jerred hoped that Raven could redirect him.

Stig sent scouts ahead to see if the top of the pass could be reached before more snowfall blocked it. His mission was to join Eskil and combine their forces against the rabble that lived below. Mounds dedicated to the unspoken should mark his passage. They would strike, but not turn back. Ottfried would follow and sacrifice and riches would be theirs.

His men were gone quite some time, but returned before he could send more in concern.

They reported the pass clear, but for some reason they could not explain, it felt as if eyes looked down on them from the cliffs. They were very leery of traveling though it. Who could be watching? They had searched, but found nothing.

"It is the unspoken who watch us in battle. They are as anxious as we to fall on the weaklings below storms, anxious as we to savor the sacrifice of the unbelievers. Anxious as we to feast!"

His men cheered his little speech and Stig smiled widely. They were the elite of Ottfried's forces, carnivorous and feasting on those they killed in battle with vats of raw ale. To join their ranks, a man must be able to kill one of them. Few challenged.

To be sure, Stig sent an advance party though the pass. The way was difficult, but they made it, sending back a scout to report before they made their way down the other side of the mountain. Another storm blew up and slowed his progress, but eventually he reported back to Stig that all was well.

Elated, Stig moved his force up the pass. He was nearly to the summit when the Lua struck. The repeating crossbow bolts fell like heavy snow and riddled his troop with death. His attempts to rally the men failed, they were stunned and scattered. Others ran back the way they came and were set upon by screaming warriors. They were shocked that some were women, welding sword or bludgeon.

But the followers of the unspoken were fighters after all. To fail the unspoken was not an option, so the battle quickly became pockets of fierce resistance and running skirmishes up and down the pass. From his vantage point on the cliffs, Jerred sent his messages to the captains and watched the battle through the strange rod Raven gave him. It was carved from hard wood and capped at both ends with thick glass. He was astonished that the fighters appeared practically at his feet when he looked through it. Jerred ached to fight but the commanders were adamant about his safety. They realized his worth as a leader and did not want to risk losing him and thus the support of the lords who sent aid. As before, the Lua continued to pick off the fighters. The wind died and occasionally longbow shafts sang down the pass to stake fighters to the ground. If necessary, a final death stroke from sword or axe was swiftly delivered.

Jerred had held back some of his fighters, now with afternoon approaching he sent word for them to join the fighting. Warriors burst screaming from cave and cliff to fall upon Stig's men like a hammer blow.

Then a shriek, like nothing ever heard before echoed off the cliffs and Jerred's heart stuttered with joy, and fear. Raven and Chi were cutting and tearing their way up the mountain. A roar went up and Ullric appeared, black with the dried blood of his foes and singing the death song as he killed.

Jerred watched in amazement as the NorBlad clans tore through the ranks of unspoken. Today was their redemption before the ones forsaken. Today they would be worthy of Tor's halls. Today they would leave none alive.

Some of the unspoken tried to reach the mouth of the pass, Ottfried must be told. But they were cut off by injured NorBlad, to weak to climb higher but not so wounded they could not kill. They sold their lives gratefully, the chance of redemption for their superstitions not to be missed.

As night fell, Jerred pulled his fighters from the field. There were few of the unspoken left and more and more of the NorBlad were lost in berserk rages, even smashing the dead again and again. He searched out Ullric among the bodies writhing in the pass and saw him chase a man down and take his head. He screamed defiance and hacked his way up and down the pass rendering bodies to so much paste of blood, snow and mud. Jerred kept his troops away, though they were anxious to check for survivors among their people. He did not want to kill Ullric. Would he have to do it? Could Ullric be stopped?

No one saw Raven's swift passage in the lowering light. He used the hilt of a broadsword to smack Ullric in the head. Chi appeared at his side and permitted the big body to be slung over his back. They made their way across the pile of corpses and moaning bodies to the cliff where Jerred stood watch. With some difficulty and a little help from Jerred's captains, he got Ullric to the top.

They struggled to move the heavy body into the cave.

"I knew you would not want this one to die Jerred. You should bind him until you know that his mind is still his own."

"I thank you Raven. Sometimes I believe you read minds. I did not want to have to kill him after all he as done for me."

"He has been revenged Jerred, but hear me. From the night he spoke to his people to urge them to fight once more, Ullric has not been as you knew him. The rage took him and he killed many who rejected his plea. All that fell away were killed. There were so few, mostly children, willing to fight. Chi and I stopped the ones who would warn Ottfried and his hall was burned. Ullric took his head and I have it as proof for your allies that he is dead."

Jerred nodded and turned himself to the task of securing Ullric.

"If he is mad..."

"Then I will release him to his god's halls. They say there is feasting and care is given by the wives of their god. He believes this, so death would only give him happiness."

"Do you not believe in the gods, Raven?"

Raven busied himself cleaning blood from the body and smearing his own healing salve on the worst of Ullric's wounds.

"The Thanatu believe all was created by a great burst of powerful light, akin to more suns than can be counted. They believe all things are one and harm against another diminishes that light. The Light is Life."

"But they are the most notorious fighters known to us."

"That is why they almost never leave their lands and only fight to defend it or their lives. They have a code of justice that is considered unbreakable. Before I was permitted to join their ranks, even after Chi chose me, I had to swear an oath to never use my sword to take the blood of an innocent, unless it was to ease their suffering. A part of the light must never be trapped, only returned to the beginning. Do not fear. I have done what I could before coming to you."

The two of them covered Ullric in blankets and settled him on a pile of furs.

Exhausted Raven settled by the fire and drank strong tea. He refused all food with a grimace of disgust.

The young lord mulled over the words of the Thanatu. After the first battle when he was told of Raven killing the fallen he had been appalled. The wounded should be tended even if dying. Later, he was not so assured. He heard the screaming of warriors held down while limbs were removed or the crying for mothers to save them from suffering mortal wounds, sometimes taking days to die. It was strange how his views had clouded, considering he spent very little time with the Thanatu. Perhaps it was the horror of war itself. He hoped to never again stand aside while people died. He hoped to never go to war again.

Chi surprised Jerred stepping from the shadows. How the animal came to climb the cliff side caused him no little surprise. He thought that line of questioning should not be addressed, as a shiver ran up his back. Raven left the fireside and lay down. Chi stood over him, appearing to sleep as the survivors of the fighting began reporting in earnest. Dawn was breaking before Jerred felt it safe to sleep.

Most of the fighters slept for one or even two days. They awoke stiff and surly, a few grieving for lost comrades. Ullric woke once in the first night. He did not know where he was but there were no screams and no scent of blood. He drifted away after a time, plagued by aches and stinging pains. His head felt twice its size and hurt until tears ran from his eyes. He was grateful for unconsciousness.

The Lua stood watch over the pass. Word came that Raven sought the last of the Wolf pack. The Lua went out and found Noak and Ivo dead, yet standing, rough spears driven through both their bodies. Their enemies lay hip deep around them. The Lua sent up their victory ululation at the sight. Jerred and Raven came and together broke the shafts. The Lua took the frozen bodies and wrapped them in their own tarps. As the dead from below storms were removed from the field, the search for Elika continued. Finally when they thought he was buried forever beneath the snow, his body was found beneath four unspoken, pierced by all their swords. They managed to kill him only after being dealt mortal wounds.

The surviving NorBlad said the dead would be his personal slaves in Tor's hall. The Lua wrapped him also. They waited for Ullric.

Jerred wondered if they would be forced to winter in the pass. It would be very hard and many wounded would not recover in damp caves with inadequate care. He hoped the weather would clear soon so he could move them off the mountain.

Ullric lay watching the fire. The wind screeched and sighed outside, but within the cave was a haven of peace. He felt marginally better, unaware of his bound hands and feet. He blinked and Raven was there pouring tea in a battered tankard. The pale eyes lifted and Raven rose and crossed to his side. Without a word he shifted Ullric's body and eased him to sit up. He pressed the cup to Ullric's lips. For a moment the blond just stared at him and then took a tentative sip. He tasted as it should, so he took another.

"Ullric...do you remember the fighting?"

The big blond scowled, staring hard at the Thanatu.

"What has addled your brain boy? You were fighting to, I saw you."

His voice was barely a whisper after the days of screaming.

"What is the last thing..."

"I am not witless. We killed the damned unspoken. Are any left alive? Is that why you speak to me like a spooked horse?"

"Peace Ullric, peace. There are none left and no one got out of the pass alive except a scouting party. We let them cross the mountain, but there were Lua and more men waiting for them on the other side."

"Well, we need to go quickly and make sure they are dead. I would trust no one else to catch those devils." He jerked as if to rise and discovered his bound limbs. He frowned and glared at Raven, who gazed serenely back and said nothing.

After a long silence, Ullric blinked and his body slumped.

"You feared I would harm Jerred's people. I was berserk, again?"

"Yes. We dared not risk you kill Jerred and have the people turn on you. To many would die."

"I do not feel strong enough to paddle a babe Thanatu. I would relieve myself and eat--then maybe sleep more."

"There is much time for sleeping. The storm continues, so Jerred decreed we remain sheltered in these cliffs until we can climb the summit. I hope it is soon. I do not like the cold. Ullric, your pack mates--"

Green eyes stared into his, a hard shudder wracked the big body and Ullric made a sound like a grunt, quickly choked off.

He sat quietly while Raven cut his bonds and

chaffed the numb wrists. He did not protest when he needed to lean against the Thanatu until his stiff limbs would support him. He realized that Jerred was absent to protect himself in case Ullric woke up maddened. Uneasy laughter beat at his throat, for he realized the young lord thought Raven and Chi were the only ones strong enough to kill him if he ran amok. When he could stagger on his own, Raven let him go. He welcomed the battle with the elements and filled his lungs with the icy air. He returned and squatted by the fire, eating the hot food with shaky hands.

"How long have I been sleeping Thanatu?"

"It has been five days I think. I woke you sometimes to make sure you would live. I had to hit you very hard to stop you."

"I will be glad to get off this mountain. I am sick of this stew."

"I will return to Milty's inn for a while. His cook tempts a man to excess."

"My men--died well?"

"The Lua have invoked their gods for them in your stead. They keep the bodies and have pledged them safely to the other side if you wish it. They deserve a pyre, Ullric. The Lua wish you to sing their battle song to escort them to your god's hall."

For a long time Ullric stared into the bowl. He dared not speak. The last of the Wolf pack were dead, now he was alone. His mind could not wrap itself around the concept. No one, child woman warrior remained. Raven caught the bowl when it fell from his hands. Most of them had died by the sword, thank Tor for the blessing. He left the fire, to sit in the deeper shadows facing the cave wall. Raven left after a while to report to Jerred and leave Ullric some time to grieve in peace. The Thanatu grieved with him. To have no place and belong to nothing was an all too familiar circumstance.

Hours later Raven returned with Jerred. The young lord knew no words of comfort to ease the enormity of Ullric's loss. He rekindled the flame and reheated the stew. The young lord could not wait to return to his holdings and spend the rest of the winter warm and dry. Ullric remained silent. He acknowledged no one and did not eat or drink. The Thanatu wondered if he would fall on his sword.

Jerred did not want that to happen. For all that was lost, he hoped Ullric would remain with him. He could live again, perhaps find a woman among Jerred's people and start his own pack. The thought made the young man smile sadly. Life did go on, if you allowed it.

The business of war had replaced his grief. Soon as his people were safe his losses would surely come to haunt him for many sleepless nights. He wished that time to pass swiftly.

Raven had told him of all the events leading up to

their arrival during the battle. Jerred filled many skins with the tale. The other lords would want an accounting. He would have everything copied by his scribes and dispatched to the midlands. The broken NorBlad would be too occupied with survival and squabbling among them selves to be a threat for at least a generation.

If they attempted to raid next winter, there would be another bitter surprise awaiting them. He had already contracted with the Lua for a company to return to patrol the pass. They seemed to care not what terrain or weather they worked in, as long as they were paid. The women had proved amazingly hardy, considering their size and the fact that this was the first time in memory they had ever survived in such conditions. None of their company had been lost during the campaign. Jerred's decision to use them strictly as archers kept their numbers intact.

One morning the army awoke to complete silence. The sky was clear of storm clouds, though still metal gray. The few surviving NorBlad broke trail for the people below storms. Jerred needed little encouragement to get his people moving as quickly as possible. Ullric's axe was packed with Jerred's things and Raven carried the short sword the big man used like a knife. Ullric carried supplies or wounded, whatever the Thanatu or Jerred put him to, without complaint.

It took days of struggle to gain the summit and

descend on the other side, hampered by wounded and exhaustion.

Jerred and Raven were the last to descend, watching the three survivors of the NorBlad turn back to whatever fate awaited them. Ullric had not responded to their presence or indicated in any way that he was aware of what was happening around him.

A supply train met them during the descent. So fortified, they pushed on to Jerred's holdings.

The young lord looked once more on the town and his home with wonder. It was still some miles off, but men had gone ahead to give the news that NorBlad and the dark worshipers were broken to raid no more. Already he could see townspeople waiting to take their loved ones home or hear the tales of death. The inns would welcome many once they were paid.

His gates were thrown wide to accommodate the fighters. Orders were given to supply those who wanted to immediately begin their journeys south. Food flowed from the town and his kitchens. Throughout his small domain weeping and celebration mingled as riders from the city spread the news from village to farmstead.

He asked Raven to bring Ullric to his house and the two of them settled him into a guest room he used before. Docile as a babe, he turned to the wall and slept. Without too much fuss, Chi was stabled with Jerred's horses. He spent many days just sleeping and for once was content with grains and water.

Raven organized supplies for those at the campsite and settled the few fights caused by strong drink simply by showing his face. He stayed on his feet, fulfilling Jerred's orders and everyone complied. They were too tired and uneasy in his presence to do anything else.

Jerred avoided his bed, knowing true rest would bring dreams of the past, nearly four seasons of grief, physical and mental stress. He was thin and deathly pale, with dark shadows around sunken eyes. In a moment of hysterical humor he likened himself to a white owl and his servants signed against evil. Everyone knew the owls were omens of death. Their new lord had been tried to near breaking. Guilt and relief churned in his gut. He had not bloodied his sword on the enemy, yet many praised him for wisdom beyond his years. Before they could convince him to rest, Jerred just keeled over.

When Raven made to sleep in the stables, the servants protested most violently at the insult to their lord and put him to bed. He was asleep before he could stretch out his limbs.

The wind was not screeching in his ears. He was very warm and lay on something soft. Nothing hurt--

Ullric jumped from bed, having no idea where he was.

It was long minutes before the concept of room or building entered his thought process. The candles burned low, but he gradually understood he was in the room Jerred had given him. He remembered scoffing at the comfort. Telling the boy that such things made men weak. Jerred had not been weak. These thoughts prompted Ullric to seek him out. There were no candles lit in the hallway and the small stump of wax he carried barely illuminated beyond his own hand. But he came to the door and pushed it open as quietly as he could. He crossed the large room by memory, holding his dim light over the bed. Jerred was buried beneath the covers to his eyes, snoring softly. So, he was alive. Ullric shook his head to deny the feeling that swelled beneath his heart. He left quickly and pulled the door closed behind him. For another moment he stood, unsure what to do. Fatigue still dragged his eyelids down, so he turned back to his room and tumbled gratefully into oblivion. Raven shut the door to his room. Jerred would not come to harm at Ullric's hands. The NorBlad was in his right mind, thank the Light. The mercenary could finally sleep without worry.

The following weeks were busy ones for the people of Virgilia. There were many wounded to tend, warriors in need of entertainment and pretty trinkets for them to purchase for love ones. A few would remain until after the spring thaw. They would stay snug by the fires and travel during the summer. Jerred and his right hands slept for a week between them.

Raven sat in a huge tub filled with hot water. Sweet scented lather enveloped his big frame. He slipped a little lower in the water, closed his eyes and relaxed against the rim of the tub. Carefully, as if sneaking up on an enemy, his hands massaged his chest and tugged on the rings in his nipples. Slowly he worked his way to the hard pole standing between his thighs. He lathered, stroked it and tugged on the ring. The leisurely pace kept him just short of completion for nearly an hour.

Below him servants were setting out an evening meal and his belly anticipated that pleasure as well. The door to the bathing chamber opened and Ullric stalked in. He scowled at Raven.

"Are you ever coming out of here? First you insist on bathing and then you stink the place up like some temple dweller."

Raven just smiled and lazily continued the ministration to his body. He was very close to release. He would not let Ullric cheat him of earned pleasure.

"Just because you stink is no reason to give up my turn in the bath."

"I do not stink. I--"

"You wear next to nothing in this devilish weather. You have nothing I do not. We are men. Why must I leave?"

Ullric opened his mouth, but said nothing.

"Give over Ullric. I--have--not had time to rest since sunrise two days past. The other tub is full. Take you bath and be quiet."

Raven sighed, closed his eyes and slipped a fraction deeper into the water. For a few seconds he was still, then his big hands returned to their meticulous journey over his body.

Ullric stomped over to the other tub and stepped in. The water was only lukewarm and the hard milled soap was roughly made and not scented like the stuff the Thanatu wallowed in.

Jerred lived for a time in the midlands and brought the notion of constant bathing back with him. He had built this addition to his hold and spent the good parts of many mornings here. Ullric had always scoffed at the notion. Fresh water was too rare a commodity were he came from. Sometimes the winter snows were tainted causing illness and death just falling from the sky. Braving freezing temperatures to heat water for bathing made no sense at all. When Raven discovered the room, he was to say the least, very happy. Jerred found humor in his enthusiasm and the servants, particularly the women, were happy to oblige the fighter's needs. So twice a day now, instead of one, a roaring fire warmed the bathing chamber. Every night before last meal Raven had a bath. Sometimes quickly and other times he wallowed like a pig in mud for an hour or more.

However, tonight Jerred was having dinner to say goodbye to the last of his captains and a few surviving second sons of nobility. Wounds healed, they were returning to their homes carrying dispatches to their families and masters. He insisted the duo appear. Ullric thought it might offend Jerred if he came to his table, after rounding up scattered horses and hunting all day, without a bath. He washed quickly, even his hair and was already drying his body, when a low moan rose up from the other tub.

He could not stop himself from looking over as Raven's body jerked and tensed in release.

Ullric put on new boots and breeches made from buckskin. The pants annoyed him, but Jerred insisted he could not roam among the women in a loincloth and little else as he had done most of the winter. People had still been wary of the grieving man's temper to insist he conform to their customs. The blonde giant often wondered if he would know himself in a season's time. He chaffed under the concessions that curbed his normal habits. He refused to wear woolen shirts, common attire in the mountains, and since every one made for him split when he flexed a muscle, Jerred had given in, exasperated.

Raven rinsed himself off with clear water sitting

in buckets by the tub. Ullric shook his head in disgust. The man should have been a fish.

He was compelled to stay and watched in amazement as Raven oiled his body with a small sliver of some greasy looking substance. The air filled with this new scent but the combination was not displeasing.

"You prepare yourself like--like a woman waiting for a lover." He had almost said Grete's name out loud. Pain choked him at the memory.

Raven growled at Ullric, giving him a piercing look. He took his time completing the rubdown and dressed quickly in black wool pants and a worn black silk shirt. Strange snake-like creatures were embroidered on the collar and cuffs. He stomped into his black boots then brushed his straight black hair until it lay flat and gleaming across his shoulders.

"Come then. I thought you were hungry."

"I am always hungry. Jerred feeds us, but it is not enough."

"I will take you to Milty's again. He will stuff you until you cannot leave the table. Eat little, then we will go."

"I have no patience to sit and listen to fawning rabble at Jerred's table."

Raven gave the big NorBlad a look.

"These men will go back to their families and speak of what happened here. Now that the people of storms are no threat, many may think to add Jerred's mountains to their holdings."

"Ten devils take them! The man has saved their ungrateful hides and now--"

"That is why we go to dinner. Let them know what will happen--"

"I tell you what will happen! I will happen. I will leave none alive--"

Ullric face reddened and he crowded Raven in his anger.

The Thanatu did not back down or touch the angry warrior.

"At the table tonight sit near him. Bring your axe and--"

"--break them in half!"

"No big fool, just look like you will."

"Do you mock me little man?"

Raven sighed long and deep.

"Ullric, Jerred is in no danger, at present. But all must know that you will be willing to fight for him. Word is spreading that you are a mad fighter who cannot be killed. Many are fearful this is true. Let them--"

"I do not need you to tell me how to make men afraid. If you wring their necks, they are afraid."

He stomped down the corridor, intent on obtaining his axe, anger barely in check.

Raven fetched his small blades and strapped them

to his back. A trip to Milty's for a full belly and a few tankards was probably a good idea. They should go now and miss dinner. He sighed once more as he stomped down the stairs. He just agitated a fearsome warrior who may go berserk at the table.

He did not understand how he came to be the nursemaid to a grown man. Ullric treated Jerred like a younger brother, true, but everyone else called Raven's name if they needed to impart bad tidings to the man. Over the season since their return, Jerred had turned his efforts to fortifying his right to hold the lands around him and make sure his people were well fed and content. He was not fool enough to think that a war won would keep his home intact. Dedric's traitorous actions were proof of that. The Wolf Clan had always brought him victory, yet he turned on them like a rabid beast. Raven was anxious to leave and he had no idea if Ullric would remain, so he gladly paid the Thanatu to stay through the winter.

The fearsome duo had enforced his claim against midland bandits, expecting depleted forces and easy pickings. Tired and angry to be tested again, the mercenaries called for volunteers and harried the bandits beyond the borders of Jerred's land. A minor noble to the west had thought to lay claim to land lying fallow while most of the villagers had gone to the fighting. Ullric and Raven took the land with the angry farmers at their backs clamoring for blood. Jerred sent the man and his family to the south in chains for insurrection. The midland lords were very careful in choosing a replacement to take over the traitor's holding. They wished to avoid fighting Jerred for so small a matter after discovering the near indestructible fighters remained at his side.

Jerrod's guests were already seated when Ullric and Raven arrived. All conversation ceased as the armed men sat at the table to the left and right of the young lord's chair.

Jerrod carefully schooled the astonishment from his face. Ullric and Raven were armed! It was not customary to attend the lord's table in such a fashion, even in these mountains far from more civilized lands. Whatever had occurred to cause them to do such a thing? Never the less, he seated himself and commanded the servants to serve as if nothing was amiss. When the tankards were topped off he glanced at the two men giving them a signal to enlighten him to the current threat.

Surprisingly, it was Ullric who stood and faced the ten men seated at the table.

"You know the outcome of our battles. You know the cost. Many of you return so late to your homes due to grievous wounds and the trade talks and treaties that ache the head of a fighting man. I may be the last of the

NorBlad to ever be seen in this land. My people are broken and raid no more. But hear me well lowlanders, go back to your masters and fathers with this vow hanging over your heads. If hand is ever raised against this hold, as the NorBlad was swept before me, so shall you be!"

His eyes blazed with the remnants of berserker rage. He forced each man to meet his eyes and then sat, his big gnarled hands trembling slightly on the tabletop. Every man knew Ullric ached for someone to challenge him.

Just when Jerrod thought to began the meal Raven left his seat.

The mercenary raised a keen blade and drew it across his palm. Bright blood filled the cut. The Thanatu flexed and his life's essence spilled into the tankard before Jerrod and the one held by the sullen NorBlad. He sat down and pressed his lips over the wound, his eyes on Jerrod. White faced the young man reached for the tankard, his eyes never leaving the warrior now gazing into his. He drank the wine in two long swallows, all the time wondering if he was participating in some dark magic. For Raven it was a mark of trust that the man emptied the cup without question. Ullric scowled at Raven, clamped down on the tankard and poured the bloodied liquor down his throat, not willing to be bested by the younger man.

If the Thanatu put a spell on them, he would snap his neck.

"Hear me. Jerrod of Virgilia and Ullric are now of my blood. I will--avenge them."

He sat down. Everyone stared. A shiver raced down more than one back at the memory of this silent assassin slipping by armed guards just to kill them.

It was a very subdued dinner. Everyone complimented Jerrod at its end. They praised his leadership and thanked him for his extended hospitality, all with one eye on the glaring blond and the quiet man so focused on his food. When the sun rose, they would all be deep in the forests headed south.

Epilogue

Jerrod stood in the yard, watching his brother ride away.

Ullric had grown increasingly surly as the spring thaw dragged to its end. He came to the decision for the safety of Jerrod's people he must leave, at least for a time. Surprisingly, he decided to ride with Raven. The word had come of hostilities rising between cities in the midlands and the mercenary was anxious to be gone. Chi had spent more and more time alone. He hunted for pleasure. Raven feared "not horse" natural contempt for men would lead to trouble. Jerred knew he would miss them. For all his bluster and temper, Ullric had found some ease from the grief that nearly drove him to madness. You could not lose all that you loved, raise war against your own people and survive with soul intact.

Jerrod had his responsibility. It kept him going through the winter of grief. Thanks to all those who died and the unrelenting retribution of Ullric, peace held sway over the mountains. He hoped that in time his brother would return to enjoy that peace. He did not want to see Ullric welding his battleaxe again.

One thing Jerrod promised himself, to never relax his vigilance. A mercenary's life was a risky one and though sworn, Ullric and Raven may not be alive to ride to his aid. He would not, could not fail as his father and grandfather before him. Resolute, the young man turned away to visit Mabe, a seamstress Raven had enthusiastically recommended. It was time for new clothes and preparing for the endless visits the lowland nobles would insist on. They would seek to weld alliances with offers of marriage. Raven assured him Mabe would outfit him well.

AMBER TRAIL

Shoving the surprised farmer to the ground, Migui leaped over his body to gain the ditch beyond the dusty road. Filthy rags flapped around him. The stink diverted the angry farmer and other travelers from snatching the thief off his feet. A loud bellow rose up behind him charging his heart to over drive. Migui jumped into the ditch to scramble up the other side. Thick dust slipping beneath his churning feet made the ascent nearly impossible. A shadow fell across his path, the big chestnut gelding his victim was riding landed before him. His startled fall back into the ditch saved his neck. The battle-axe swept through the air, the edge just nicking Migui's face. He shrieked in terror, believing his head severed. His screams were abruptly cut off when Ullric lifted his writhing body into the air by his throat. Migui was shaken until most of the dust that layered him was once again returned to earth. He was barely conscious when his loot was ripped from the inner pockets along with the filthy coat. The NorBlad raged at him in the heathen tongue of his people, but Migui needed no translation to understand his displeasure. With a roar Ullric tossed the thief over his horse's neck, nodding in satisfaction when he landed with a solid thump far from ditch and road. The lump of probable broken bones did not move.

"I think that one will not be lifting purses for some time."

Raven leaned on the horn of his saddle, unable to hide his amusement at the circumstances.

Ullric did not understand thievery. No warrior would sneak and crawl like vermin to take from another. If you wanted it you challenged and fought until the other was dead or you were. Raven had been unable to make Ullric understand that just because you could kill a weaker man, did not give you the right to take what was his. Not only were you a thief but a murderer as well. Ullric had lived in a world where the strongest survived and he interpreted that credo literally. During the months they traveled together, Raven more often than not stood between some hapless fool and Ullric's axe. He grinned as the pile of rags began to scuttle across the dusty ground, the desperate wheezing and groaning clearly audible.

Ullric turned and would have ridden after his prey, but Raven laughed and reminded him of the city they were approaching rife with strong ales and women. Ullric threw one more black scowl at the retreating thief and followed Raven back onto the road and the milling travelers. Most of them made quick work of leaving plenty of room around the NorBlad. His green eyes blazed with malice. As usual Raven ignored his bad attitude, eventually drifting into the light connection with Chi, which sustained him.

Ullric scowled at the surroundings. People clogged the roadway on foot, some herding long legged folly birds, an absurd creature that squawked and staggered around like a drunken man. They were nearly bare, having sparse red and white feathers, short stubby wings and long skinny green legs. The only good thing, they tasted wonderful roasted, baked or fricasseed.

Rickety wagons loaded with hay, various grains and vegetables bounced along, their drivers shouting at stubborn asses and even slower oxen. Periodically one would lose a wheel or break an axle causing a major crush and much milling about as confused angry people attempted to leave the road to go around the blockade. More than a bit difficult since there were deep ditches bordering both sides.

Prosperous merchants had caravans on the road loaded with fine fabric, lumber, wines and the most precious of merchandise, water.

The thief was the last straw in a series of annoyances that had plagued Ullric since this new leg of their journey began.

He had taken a tavern wench to his bed in the last

town at the edge of the midlands. Later a group of drunken idiots ran him to ground demanding he pay for the time he spent with her. He told them what they could do with their demands and, of course, had to kill them all. Raven and Chi watched the altercation, the mercenary teasing him for hours about his choice of bed mates. Then, another inebriated fool attempted to run him through because he was some fabled demon. Raven took this incident more seriously and threatened to end the life of any who thought to attack their company. Ullric cursed him. He was no stripling needing someone to hold his hand. Chi snorted and Ullric's face heated. He hated the beast's superior air. But Chi cared not a wit for the berserker's feelings and trotted away leaving the man to stew.

Ullric snapped the wrist of a well-heeled foot pad trying to cut one of their bags loose from the packhorses just this morning. Did he look like an easy victim, or was everyone in this new country an idiot?

Disgusted with Raven's "you must not kill just because you can" attitude and with himself for going along with it, the scowling warrior urged his horse through the crowd hoping just one more fool would give him cause. Raven smiled listening to the shouts of consternation as the people scurried from the horse's path. No one demanded payment for the few folly birds oblivious to the warhorse's great hooves. The big chestnut had been a gift from Jerred, one of three bred from a farmer's big draft horse and a war mount gifted by one of the middle ranges nobles when Jerred's father was lord. He had the stamina to carry the big NorBlad on his wide back. Enraged bellows and the clash of steel never usurped his serenity and his big hooves had already dented many a head in skirmishes the duo never failed to encounter.

The pair had traveled south after leaving Jerred's hold, Raven anxious to get to warmer climes. They passed through the mountains without difficulty stopping only once to discourage a group of heavily armed men from continuing their journey toward Jerred's lands. Raven staked their heads on pine poles and decorated the bridge the men had attempted to cross with them. It was a sign the Thanatu were known for displaying on the borders of their territory.

Ullric found the new country interesting. There was very thick forest with moss and vine covered bridges. Each crossed deep canyons of rapid water. Raven told him the people that built the log crossings disappeared long ago. No one knows who they were but travelers still kept the bridges clear of growth to make the journey quicker to and from the middle ranges.

Water was abundant so once they reached the lower elevations; Raven took the opportunity to swim in the chill lakes and rivers. His not so subtle hint regarding the big man's courage demanded Ullric learn. Before they left the mountains he could keep himself afloat and paddle across a lake, much to Raven's amusement. He did not comment on the grimly determine man's resemblance to a drowning dog as he struggled along.

Finally they left the snow-capped peaks and Ullric was shocked to see a valley covered with bright yellow gold. Raven let him live the fantasy for a moment, then rode on to the edge of the field. Flowers, miles and miles of flowers. Ullric cursed him, while Raven laughed out loud at his disillusionment. The big fool thought men would leave gold lying about? They camped for the night. Raven advised him to hobble his horse and strap on the feedbag until they left the area. The tiny golden bells were poisonous to animals. Had Ullric realized not one honey maker, bird or beast moved over the miles of fragrant blossoms? Ullric advised the Thanatu that no, he had not noticed because he had never seen a honey maker and flowers did not grow where he came from.

Dangerous or not, the flowers were pretty and harvested for sale in some of the midland cities. They were considered signs of true devotion and given as gifts between lovers. No mention was made of the untraceable poison that could be distilled from them, this fact known only to a few sorcerers, assassin guilds and the most powerful of the nobles. Ullric's incredulous stare caused more laughter. Indeed, men always proved themselves fools. No woman's bed was worth risking death by flower, what idiocy!

It was a four-day journey around the flowers even with the forced pace Ullric insisted on. He was not going to sleep anywhere close to poison plants and that was final. It galled him that Raven found his every action a source of amusement. He didn't kill the insolent Thanatu because he was unaware of the lands and customs they would encounter. But one day--

Their journey through the middle ranges was constantly stalled by invitations from nobles curious about their business and anxious for news about Jerred. Men, who would never have spoken directly to the mercenary, now courted his presence and fearfully allowed the NorBlad to their tables. Ullric ate huge quantities and drank twice as much. He spoke little and observed everything with a grim mien. Late in the night he would watch as Raven wrote down their observations. The dispatches were sent to Jerred, but by what method, Ullric did not know. Occasionally, Raven would accept a job guarding a caravan or some landowner's holdings as they wandered further away from the mountains. They always made quick work of the rabble. Ullric was already missing the colder regions and Jerred, much to his surprise.

So here they were, the middle of the summer season, riding through a land devoid of plant life and water. Dust covered everything in powdery layers after one of the many windstorms. The change had been an abrupt one. Raven told him a ridiculous tale of sorcerers and be spelled cities. The cursed people remained tied to the land dependent on outsiders for sustenance. They drew metal from the earth to trade. Ullric scoffed at the notion. Men always blamed magic for their own failings. His experience proved magic was an excuse to defend cowardice and greed.

Ullric could taste the ale waiting at the first tavern they came to. That is if Raven would buy. He did not have many coins in his pouch, having spent them on ale and attempts to master games of chance. He never paid for women, especially not the skinny wenches that populated the taverns or roadside hovels passing for inns. There was barely any meat on them for a man to hang onto. If he feared breaking the wench she was no use to him. Raven warned him that many of the women were diseased and he should be wary. So the first time he found a woman of reasonable health and strength, he had to kill her so called husband and his "brothers" two days later. He frowned as he wondered if she actually plotted to ensnare her whore master within the reach of his axe. He shook his head banishing the thought. No use entertaining the possibility. She was now free to find another "husband" or not.

Once again he rode beside the Thanatu, noticing Raven was at rest, relying on Chi to watch the people churning around them. Finally, the waning sun found them stalled on the road before the walled metropolis.

The city gates were open, high-reinforced sheets of iron! He had never seen so much metal used for such a thing. The walls were some kind of stone much the color of the earth they rode upon. Workers could be seen pushing barrels on wheels, stopping to fill cracks and breaks in the wall with some liquid version of the pale stone. Men dressed in bright cloaks of orange and black guarded the gates, wearing dark metal helms and chest guards over dark tunic and breeches. They wore short and long sword, plus daggers at their waists. Some of them searched baggage and wagons while others stood aside with drawn weapons.

Raven had explained the cities were governed by an hereditary nobility. Saboteurs and spies were a constant problem as one city attempted to undermine trade with the outlying lands. There was little reason for open warfare. Horses and other animals were kept only by owners rich enough to support the exorbitant amounts of money it cost to import their feed. At least five hundred leagues separated the cities across the barren terrain. Assassination attempts, mining accidents and a steady flow of information buying and selling occurred instead of war.

By the time they arrived at the gate, Raven was alert and scanning the crowd. One of the guardsman hurried away at the sight of them. Raven watched him go with a faint smile. Ullric kept his eyes straight ahead to avoid challenging one of the overdressed follies to battle. He thought they should be roasting in the ridiculous armor and capes. The Thanatu waited patiently, ignoring Ullric's grumbles at the delay.

"Hail Aja", a helmed figure called. He was tall and slim dressed as the others except the dagger at his waist was encrusted with jeweled stones of onyx and amber.

"My lord will be glad of your return. Annoyances are many since you last resided here."

"Hail Jirair. My eyes delight in your presence."

Ullric rolled his eyes at the womanish greeting.

"As do mine, old friend. You are unscathed. It is good."

Raven dismounted and wrapped his big arms around the slim Captain of the Guard. Jirair had taken the chance to hire him many years ago, before his sojourn with the Thanatu. It had been a profitable event for both. Jirair filled his purse and served his lord well enough to eventually rise to Captain. He was content with his lot, thanks to the dark haired young one. He laughed into the shoulder and pushed away from his brawny captor.

"I do believe you have added another stone or two to this bulk you carry, Aja". He laughed at the faint blush that touched Raven's face. He had long made his feelings known and Raven took no offense at his frank appraisal.

"Oh, that is Ullric. He is not has heavy as he looks." Raven diverted Jirair's attention to the scowling barbarian. The captain laughed and clapped Raven on the back.

"Hail Ullric. You must be gifted indeed to ride with Aja. Perhaps there will be profit for you also in my lord's employ."

Ullric just glared. He wanted a tankard and off the twice cursed road.

"Forgive me, mighty warrior. I have not seen my friend in many years. You will abide with me, Aja. My servants will see to your needs."

"Your courtesy to one beneath your notice is a noble act Jirair Guerdon."

It was the Captain's turn to scowl at the Thanatu.

"Speak not as a servant, Aja. But for you I would still be searching baggage at the gate. Come, no more this. You are a guest in my home and of greater value than the lord I serve."

Turning back to the gates, Jirair lead the duo through, denying the soldiers desire to search their packs. People made way for them, a few bowing and calling out to

Jirair. The main roads through the city were wide to accommodate all the wagons. Buildings were populated with taverns, inns and metalworker's shops, servants and apprentices living above them. Smoke and steam drifted above the street. The cacophony of hammers against metal was deafening. Hawkers called visitors to take lodging and wenches quoted their prices from the upper floors echoed within the alleys of sometimes six storied buildings. Ullric had never seen edifices where people lived stacked upon each other like goods in a storage shed. Animals squealed and brayed. People yelled, cursed and occasionally a fight would tumble out into the street. The orange and black cloaks of the city guard could be seen moving through the crowds, quickly stamping out the violence. The farmers and traders flowing into the streets added to the din.

Eventually Jirair turned off the main thoroughfare and entered another metal gate locked and guarded by two soldiers. Another duo looked out from the top of the expanse, which connected the gate to buildings on either side housing a troop. Ullric thought it interesting that the men guarding this place lived outside the walls instead of within. Laundry hung from windows and someone was playing a wheezy horn to the raucous laughter of their audience.

The guards saluted the Captain and refrained from commenting on his guests. The gates banged shut behind them and the silence was startling. Small houses of the same material as the outer walls lined these streets. The doors were metal, some aged to a green patina. Heavy metal shutters anchored the windows for sealing out the dusty air during storms. Most had covered porches with reclining couches for resting and small tables for refreshment.

"My house is within the next square, Aja. When you last visited I was still in the barracks waiting for the old captain to retire, now I have taken wives and have children."

"My heart fills with joy at your good fortune Jirair. Few have I met who deserved it more."

"It is to you I owe this fortune. My heart is glad for I never expected to return in any measure my appreciation. I trust Ullric, you have found good fortune in meeting my friend."

Ullric grim face tightened with bad memories. Jirair's hand came to rest on his sword.

"Forgive me, warrior. I meant no offense to a guest and companion to Aja."

"You offer shelter Jiair. I would not spill your blood today."

He urged his horse ahead, even though he had only a vague notion where to go. The captain raised an eyebrow at that remark, turning his gaze to Raven.

"It is an unpleasant tale Jirair. All that gives a man

reason to continue is lost to him forever. I can say no more. Ullric is from the northern mountains and one day his story will find its way to your ears."

"I will walk on soft slippers around him Aja. He will find peace within my walls."

"Ullric is plain speaking. He will not break his word. He will not spill your blood today. "

Nothing else was said. Soon they arrived at a larger house surrounded by a walled barren yard. Jirair directed them through an arch breaking up the plain wall and up the few steps to the porch. Stone benches with red pillows were under the windows along side the carved tables. He entered the double metal doors and flung them wide. Raven and Ullric followed, war bags slung across their shoulders. The entry hall was cool, the ceilings high. In contrast to the dull gray outer walls, the interior was a blaze of white washed surface edged in filigree designs of scarlet and blue.

"Jin, Jivin", Jirair called, pulling his helm from the matted dark red hair curled above his ears.

"We have quests. Quickly, quickly."

Two slim figures draped in bright cloth hurried into the hall followed by four servants dressed in dull homespun.

"Jin, Jivin calm yourselves", he admonished over their enthusiastic kisses. "We must provide comfort and entertainment for Aja and his companion Ullric."

The woman lay aside the gold mesh veil covering her head and shoulders.

"Behold Jin first wife of my house. Her sacrifice and loyalty honors my lord. She has gifted me with sons and a daughter to delight the future."

She smiled brightly and bowed low turning to her husband and signing. She had wide blue eyes and perfumed wavy waist length blonde hair smoothed into a green band around her head. The lightweight cotton dress brushed the floor and covered her arms to the wrists. Many gold bracelets jangled on her arms.

"Jin says you are welcome and a blessing on our house. This is Jivin, second wife. His sacrifice and loyalty honors my lord. He has tended the birth of all my children and they are healthy and firm in limb. His knowledge has insured death is a stranger to us. In many generations my family has never attracted a healer. We are twice honored by his sacrifice."

Jivin lowered his golden veil and bowed low. He blushed as he gazed upon the two giants before him and smiled. His hair was oiled, perfumed and clung to his head and shoulders in red ringlets. His eyes were blue and his pale skin was covered in a similar cotton dress. Gold, copper and silver bracelets encircled his slim wrists. He also signed to Jirair who burst into laughter and signed to both his spouses. Jin playfully pushed the grinning men aside and approached Raven and Ullric. Signing slowly she urged them to follow her.

"My servants Jabir, Jaja, Jade and Jarita. Whatever you need they will provide. All are accomplished in the sexual arts and from the smiles on their faces will be very willing to serve. Go and let my family care for you. Jabir and I will see to your animals. Yes, I know Aja. Your magical beast I will not touch. His care is for you alone. Even here we know of Thanatu. Perhaps you will enthrall us with the tale how this came to be." So saying the captain left the house with a smiling curly haired blonde on his heels to walk the animals around to the stables. Jabir signed something to his master and Jirair's laughter echoed around the yard.

Ullric followed the family and Raven through airy rooms decorated with murals on the walls to a curtained enclosure containing a wide stone platform covered in bright quilted spiced pillows and comforters of quilted satin. Raven immediately protested their hospitality.

"Jin, Javin we cannot take your bed. It is not our wish to intrude. We are worthless wanderers. A place in your stables is enough."

Jin started an agitated series of gestures, obviously demanding he accept their humble offerings. She bowed and signed, Javin patting Raven's arms in a not so consoling gesture. Ullric watched the ritual go on with rapidly unraveling patience. He was tired and hungry and wanted a tankard of ale!

The low rumble of his companion's stomach caused Raven to bring his reluctant acceptance of the bed to a close. Jin and Javin smiled however and happily went off with the servants to bring refreshment.

"When does all this jabber end. I could drink a river and eat two oxen."

"Put your bag here." Raven directed as he crossed the room and sat his bags on a bench. "They will return with plenty to feed us and then we will be washed with probably the last of their water ration for the week. For the remainder of our stay we will be oiled daily to keep clean. Hear me Ullric, I will not allow these gentle souls to be insulted. We must share the bed and eat everything they give us. Jirar and his wives will sleep with the servants as long as we stay. You must refuse everything they offer and allow them to beg you to accept. It is custom here. I do not understand it but I always follow it. Before you finish the last morsel on your platter refuse it and permit them to cajole you. It will honor the house. When the lord sends for us we must appear promptly. Follow my lead. If the job is right you will leave here with a heavy purse and the lord will favor you when and if you ever return."

Ullric grunted in response, but before he could say more the servants rushed into the room and set great platters of food on a table in the corner. The northerner's stomach growled fiercely making the three servants giggle. He scowled at them and cursed Raven. Feeling stupid he crossed to the bed and sat on the edge his arms folded across his chest.

"I have decided, I will not eat."

Raven snorted at the bad acting and hide his grin behind his hand. The servants rushed to the blonde giant and timidly began to pet his shoulders and chest. They gestured to the table and when all effort failed kissed his dusty face and tried to pull his bulk off the bed.

The amused Thanatu pushed Ullric to his limit. He jumped up, scattering servants and stalked across the room planting himself at the table. The carved bench groaned beneath his weight causing even more consternation among the servers. Jaja pressed him to wash his hands and face from a bowl of beaten copper. Jade and Javita rushed to fill the empty platter before him with slabs of roasted meat, thick gravy and hot flat bread. A large goblet was filled, not with the ale he craved but a light delicate wine. After much pleading the servants got him to taste it. They actually hugged and kissed him in delight when he drank it down demanding more. He finally tucked into the platter and the trio sighed with relief. Raven finally let go and laughed out loud. He realized he had laughed more in the last few months watching Ullric stomp through his territory than in his entire life. Ullric would kill him if he ever voiced the thought, which caused him to laugh again. Shaking his head Raven went to settle Chi.

Hours later Raven lolled in the family bath. The captain and his wives washed him. The happy servants scrubbed every inch of the blond barbarian. After a through rinsing the men were moved to the bed where they were oiled and massaged until sleep claimed them. The tired family staggered off exhausted, but assured of their guest's comfort. The servants could not stop speculating on the giants sleeping in the next room. On the morrow Jirair would bring his children from visiting Jin's family home for Aja's blessing.

Sun rarely pierced the gray haze, which covered the barren land plagued by dust storms. Ullric woke in the dim light, knowing Raven awakened the same moment his breathing changed. He turned over to find the Thanatu gazing at him across the wide space.

"Why are they mute Thanatu."

"Men who claim to rule over others do many things I do not understand. If a soldier rises in the ranks to the lord's attention, he makes an oath of loyalty offering the life of his family for betrayal. Any wishing to join with him may voluntarily have their throats cut to insure they never betray him or their lord under torture. It is not required, but considered a great honor if a wife would submit to the knife. Jirair's household is many times blessed. So many gold bracelets means his wife is a daughter of nobility and much loved by her husband. His second wife is a healer born, a rare thing in this cursed land. His bracelets mean he serves all the people and is revered. As you can see Jirair's servants are treated well. Few such as they are permitted to wear metal. The copper bracelets tell everyone of their lord's favor. By giving up their voices it shows he is an exceptional master. The security of the entire city and metal is his responsibility. No other captain before him has had that honor."

"It is a dangerous thing, I think, that your friend is shown such loyalty."

"Indeed it may cause envy but it also assures the lord of his captain's devotion. The nobles were probably shamed and rushed their wives and servants to the knife to avoid suspicion by the lord. Many around him may now be mute. If the chosen mate refuses the blade, a treacherous man may rethink his plans."

Thoughts of the preceding day's laughter prompted Ullric's next comment.

"You know Jiair looks on you with lust Thanatu?"

Raven felt the blood rush to his face and turned onto his back.

"He asked when my first mission was successful if I would remain and join the troop. He made clear his attraction to me but--I cannot remain inside walls. It is a prison I can only tolerate for the time it takes to earn my gold."

Ullric could sense some stress in the Thanatu's words. Raven was indeed the closest to a fighting equal he had ever known and he did not want to spill his blood over probing into his past. The berserker rage still licked at the edges of his own mind when the past intruded. The dark warrior was an unknown quality.

"What happens if he is captured by rivals?"

"He will kill himself with poison hidden somewhere on his body. The lord swears to protect his family from that moment."

"Tell me they do not slit the throats of children." The young faces of Fox clan wavered before his eyes. His scarred hands tightened into fists.

"No, no. It is considered a great wrong to touch children. Too few are born. Jirair says to harm a child is a sin against their gods. That is why the city captain and manor soldier's families all live in a city within the city. Their noble's protectors must be protected as well. It is this way in the other five cities of the blasted plain. Trade with the people at the edge of the middle ranges is profitable. You saw little poverty within the cities and villages there because of the blasted plain. They need everything to keep their people alive, since they cannot leave for more than a span of days. Two cities further south do not fare as well as this one because the merchants charge even more that dare travel that far.

The lands beyond them are distant and untamed with three major nobles struggling for power over the other. They do not trade for metal because they have it."

"You do not expect me to believe these people will die if they abandon this dead place. You know I do not believe in magic. There is no such thing." He nearly shouted at Raven.

"Think what you will, Ullric. I have seen with my own eyes a man die before he could return. He fell into a wasting sleep and did not revive." Raven sat up just as the curtains parted and Jade entered. He wiped the frown from his face, not wanting to frighten the delicate woman. She bowed low and signed for first meal. He looked thoughtful enough that she approached him awaiting his direction.

"I think we could eat Jade, but only a little. I must not get too fat or I will not be able to work for your lord and then shame would come to Jirair."

He sighed heavily, just enough pout to his lips to capture a softhearted woman's attention. Jade hugged his neck and Raven lifted her to his lap. Her long blue-black ringlets trailed over his shoulders. Jade's eyes were pale blue with black lashes, her skin milk white. She smelled good. Raven thought he could eat later and nuzzled the soft skin behind her ear. She laughed and turned into his shoulder. Ullric watched her small hands caress Raven's hair and big back. He handled the diminutive woman with such gentleness it made Ullric uncomfortable. He would not have dared mount her as tiny as she was.

He finally got up and left the chamber his stomach growling to announce his presence to the other servants. Jaja showed him to another room and sat him down on a reclining bench. He brought in a large platter with more roasted meat and bread. This time the goblet contained a strong ale, which Ullric drank with much satisfaction. He noticed that Jaja was also dark haired and nearly identical to the woman who now pleasured Raven. This one kept his eyes lowered and blushed every time Ullric banged his goblet on the table for more ale.

Ullric did not think of men as pretty or for sex. The further he traveled into the land below storms, the stranger the customs. You might force a proven coward to show your contempt before you killed him. To lie with a man for pleasure would be very strange. He had to admit these servants were very clean and pretty, but to bed one?

The platter had been emptied twice and was being sat down for the third time when Raven came into the room. Jin and Jivin flanked him holding his big scared hands. The dresses were red today and Jivin's veil was studded with tiny rubies. It was clear he was the most vain in a household of attractive persons.

"Well no one has to wonder if you are satisfied with

your lot barbarian. Did you leave me anything, or must I go before the lord of this city weak from hunger?

"Rot you Thanatu. You eat as much as I. Besides you said not to insult them. If they must go hungry to have their honor served, then so be it."

Raven grinned and sat down at the table. Jade appeared and hurried to the table to serve the wives and Raven. She waited patiently and went to provide another platter, bringing fruit and tubers to stretch the remaining meat and bread. Eventually satisfied, Raven belched and rubbed his belly grinning at the silent satisfied laughter of his audience.

The front doors banged open and Jirair entered with a shout of his wives names. Ullric wondered if the man knew the meaning of stealth. High-pitched giggles could be heard before the slap of small bare feet heralded the arrival of the captain and four children. They ran into the arms of the wives shouting their greetings. The captain soon followed and sat at the table. The servants quickly washed dusty hands and faces and then served him fresh platters of food and water. Three boys and a girl were introduced to the warriors. They were dressed in yellow trousers and multi-colored shirts, a single gold bracelet around each wrist. Two of the boys had red hair, the oldest of them very thin, but already taller than his mothers. The remaining boy was blonde as Jin. The girl's hair was bright orange like Jivin's. She looked to be about five turns of the seasons, although tall for her age. All of the children had blue eyes and freckles. After the hugging and kissing ended, Jirair formally introduced his children to Raven and Ullric. Raven kissed their foreheads. He spoke to each in quiet tones, the little girl giggling, amused at his words.

"Remember Aja, my children. His people are legend. Few have been so favored to have his regard. He may not come again until you have children of your own. Greet him with honor in my name for good fortune will follow."

The wives reinforced Jirair's words with signs, hugs and kisses. The children were then allowed to wash and help themselves to the remainder of the food on the table.

For a time conversation revolved around the upcoming attendance of the oldest son to the academy and the younger siblings already assisting their mother in his healing duties. Raven complimented the children's accomplishments, to their bashful delight. With a sign Jirair sent his family off to other activities.

"My lord would see you on rising Aja. Your coming is an omen and he is impatient to put you to work. We fear Quellon will attempt to join one of the border lords to raid us."

Ullric spoke at his words.

"Only a fool would attempt to attack you, if what

Raven says is true your cities are all too far apart with only the cursed dust between you. All your metals would not be worth the loss of men and animals."

"This is true warrior. But many outsiders do not understand the curse that confines us. The ones who believe they do occasionally find sorcerers to attempt an ending to it."

"Then it is simple. We will take the head of the faker and the fool lord will have to think again. " Ullric snorted his contempt into his goblet as he drained another portion of ale. Jade's eyes widen as he smacked it onto the table demanding more. She hurried away giving one more awe struck glance over her shoulder. Jirair shouted with laughter.

"Ullric my servants will speak of you for many years. You eat for ten men and drank for twice more."

Ullric found himself at a loss. He honestly gave little thought to how much he consumed especially after a few tankards of ale.

"Am I taking food from the mouth of you children? Your honor is cursed if I do." His face reddened with anger and he sprang from the table.

"No, no my friend, do not fear. My lord has sent supplies in honor of your arrival. When your mission is completed my house will gain even more of the lord's blessings. We will not suffer for your appetites, but will be rewarded."

At the barbarian's wary tone Jirair was uncomfortably reminded of immense size and the menace of the Aja's friend.

"Humph. If you say so Jirair. I will just sit down-- drink my ale. Look to the Thanatu -- pay me no mind." He was grateful enough for the timely arrival of Jade and the pitcher, that he gave her a tentative smile. To his further embarrassment, she draped herself across his wide shoulders and petted him.

Jirair turned again to Raven, hiding his smile. The huge warrior was indeed, short tempered as a wildcat. Aja must truly have magic since he now commanded two such dangerous creatures.

"Does your lord still live in the old manor?"

"The one you remember is beneath the floor of the temple. His son rules. Jaap Guerdon is under much duress. Twice assassins have failed to kill him and although he has many wives, the children all die within hours of birth. A wife was taken while shopping in the market, she appeared again with no explanation and gave birth to an unspeakable thing that my lord's personal guard put to the sword. The wife is a shell that will not die."

"This is indeed a grave situation, Jirair."

"If there is more I do not know. My concerns are the mines and the city walls. It is left to my lord to enlighten you."

"There is enough ignorance of my people that the sorcerer may not understand to fear our presence."

"As you say, Aja. In this I trust my lord will heed your direction."

The remaining talk centered on Jirair's meeting his wives and life since Raven was last among them. Ullric listened with half an ear and did not dissuade Jade from eventually leading him from the room. Javita joined her and mindful of Raven's warning not to appear too eager, he forced the two women to plead and cover him with kisses before finally lying down. They took command and soon Ullric was writhing on the bed as they used their hands, lips and tongues to pleasure him. He lifted Javita to his face plundered the red curls between her legs until her essence ran down his neck. When she was limp and barely conscious he did the same for Jade who responded with many sighs of pleasure before falling asleep on his chest.

He thought to rise for another tankard when Jabir and Jaja peeked into the room. The sight forced a grin to the barbarian's face. Rising to the occasion, Ullric signed for them to come to him. Before the candle hour all four of Jirair's servants were insensible in their master's bed. Jirair and his wives smiled a lot and signed to each other furiously when they found the warrior buried under the human blanket.

Ullric slept through the evening meal. The Thanatu

found himself welcomed happily by the remaining family into the servant's quarters.

Raven woke Ullric rather early in the morning. He did not hesitate to tumble the sleepy foursome into the covers. Jin and Jivin hurried to cleanse Ullric's big body. He could not go before the lord of the city reeking of their servants loving attention. Ullric stood patiently through the oiling and scraping. He was still enjoying the lassitude of sexual gratification. He even put on long pants, standing patiently while the wives laced the rawhide strings from hip to ankle. The Thanatu's small blades were strapped to his back. So Ullric slung his battle-axe over his shoulder in its strap, settling the wide leather to rest flat against his chest.

Without another word, Raven led him from the house. The captain was riding a bay lent by the lord from his own stable. The streets were empty as ever. They left the walled compound and mingled with the busy traffic on the other side. It took some time, as Jirair traveled slowly. They eventually turned off the main road into a wide side corridor guarded along its length by heavily armed men dressed in the standard orange and black. Archers stood on the walls above them, arrows notched, keeping the trio targeted. It took six men to push the heavy gate open for them to pass through. Barracks, a blacksmith shop and various outbuildings were to their left. The scream of a hawk brought their attention to a low building with a big wire mesh cage for a second level. The hunting birds stretched their wings, snared petrified rabbits cowering on the floor and stared relentlessly at the larger prey moving about the yard. Raven shifted uneasily in the saddle. He drew a deep breath and shook the chill from his shoulders.

Jirair pulled his attention back to the party as he hailed the guards flanking the steps up to the manor doors. It was very similar to Jirair's own home, just on a grander scale. Servants rushed to tend their horses, giving the Thanatu a wide berth when Chi bared his gleaming fangs and forked tongue. The captain soothed the nervous guards with quick words.

Suddenly Chi shied away from the steps. Raven's head snapped up and he ripped first blade from his back. The third floor wall exploded and a shriek like thousands dying echoed around the yard. Chi reared to meet the thing dropping upon them. Men ran or lay smashed beneath fallen stone. Chi bit, venom gushing into the wound. Raven's sword raised and fell even as they were forced backward. He leaped from Chi's back as the struggling animal was born to earth. Then leaped once more upon the creature desperately trying to rip the horse from its chest. Ullric came in swinging his battle-axe, which bit deep. Terrified soldiers dragged Jirair, insensible from falling debris, across the yard. Some overcame their terror and rushed to kill the writhing horror in their midst. Arrows fly from the battlements, trying to find a vulnerable spot on strange dead gray hide. Black gore splattered the combatants and the stench caused many to gag and vomit. For the first time Ullric heard Raven's voice howling defiance and urged his beast to fight harder. Jaap Guerdon rushed out of the manor struggling against his own guard to see what happened.

"Help them kill it. Curse you, help them!"

His guards did leave him to add their swords to the fight and Jaap is free to draw his own weapon. Yelling defiance he rushed in and raised his sword again and again to bring the abomination down.

Thick talons struck, two men were disemboweled. The elongated neck dodged blows, jaws snap, bones were crushed. More men rushed to combat as others fell aside. Chi struggled to stand as swords and axe fell upon the roaring creature. Maddened by wounds not horse managed to drag himself far enough to rise. The air was rent by Chi's unearthly wail. He struck quick as a snake, fangs dug deep in its chest once more. The creature raised to muscled hindquarters dragging Chi into the air. He refused to relinquish his hold. Ullric's axe finally chops though shoulder muscle and one leg hung useless. Frightened men take heart; swords and arrow continued to find their mark. They were aware of

Raven's voice raised in entreaty, the language unknown to them, but the anguish obvious. He cursed, stabbed through tough hide and behind bony ridges protecting its eyes. An eye was pierced. It tried to claw the arrow out. Ten men chopped at its hindquarters. It could not strike them and the howling barbarian hacking away at its side, nor did the thing on its head stab the other eye. The ichors supporting its existence began to boil. It gagged, could not inhale and scrabbled desperately to continue the fight. Bile and foam erupted from its jaws. Raven leaped down and grabbed Ullric.

"Everybody run. Run, curse you. It dies, it dies!"

"My lord, my lord run the assassin says run."

"Go, go go. Curse you get away!"

Raven continued to scream at the men to retreat. They dragged their lord away, swearing and howling. Chi was once more earthbound, jaws burrowed into putrefying meat. He pulled and tugged against the writhing creature, his strange staccato growl raising the hair on more than one neck. Finally he backed away, staggering on bruised trembling legs. The unspeakable creature writhed in agony and fell to the ground. A shudder passed over every man when Chi screamed in defiance and victory.

This other is no more. Once again I have conquered. The one who sent you to destroy will meet destruction.

The lord ignored his shaky limbs and wildly

beating heart to issue orders for the care of the fallen and clearing of debris. Raven had noted Jiriar's absence. He finally found him inside the barracks another soldier winding a bandage around his bleeding head. A quick examination assured him, the captain had not been hit hard enough to dent his skull and was already coming around. More men were hurrying in carrying wounded. He left to see to Chi, hoping the wounds were not too severe.

"Hold, a moment Aja. Your coming was an omen of good fortune. If not for you we would be dead and this creature rampaging through my city. Anything you ask of me I will give. As long as Guerdon stands you and your companion may find sanctuary here. Never have I seen such strength and agility."

"You honor me with your attention my lord. We must speak. I will come as soon as I see to Chi's injuries. This is not over."

"As you will warrior. I would know more about this creature you call a horse. Go tend him. The rest will wait."

Raven hurried away, men passed him clearing away the evidence of battle.

Chi stood on shaky legs, the adrenaline from the fight drained away. The warrior crooned to the animal and carefully examined the torn flesh. The wounds were deep and bled freely. Warning the animal beforehand, he pressed against the injuries to force more blood to flow. There may not be water to rinse the injuries and he worried about infection.

"What may I do Thanatu? If the beast will allow me near him."

"My pack, the one marked with not horse. It has the healing potions I need."

"I will go. One of these men can guide me."

Without another word Ullric stalked away snaring a young man from the rubble. It took a moment, but he finally made himself understood. The soldier asked permission from his lord and the two left swiftly.

Jaap Guerdon sat down on his steps amazed at the events of the day.

Surely this would be more proof to the people that he was cursed above all men on the blasted plain. He scrubbed shaky hands through sweat soaked black waves. A breeze stirred in the compound and he shivered. Servants finally ventured out, but he would not go in. Someone settled a coat around his shoulders and a tankard of hot wine was held to his lips. He drank and leaned against the pillar with a sigh. He had gone to Jatara's room, hoping against sense she would awaken. For the first time his third wife moaned and thrashed about, sweat matting her golden tresses. The healer hurried in and they were attempting to bath her fevered body. She shrieked like they were slaughtering her and changed, changed right before their terrified eyes into something horrid. Struck dumb with terror, he knew he was a dead man when the thing tore through the wall. When he could force his legs to move, his personal guard attempted to keep him from the courtyard. He could hear unearthly screams. Servants ran passed, wailing about the creature killing everyone.

He made it outside to find his captain of the guard covered in blood and a blond giant bellowing a battle cry as he hacked at the creature. How could he not fight? How could he have anyone say he hid in the manor while his men were slaughtered? He barely registered the Aja hanging from the creature's head stabbing and slashing to blind it. When the horse regained his feet and screamed, Jaap thought surely it was infected by the magic. What was it that such bone melting sounds could issue forth? He began to tremble violently, once again shaking off his servants. He burrowed deeper into the coat, his thoughts despairing even in this victory. He gave permission for a guardsman to accompany the blonde on some errand and sat in the courtyard battling despair.

The livestock caretaker approached Raven, but scuttled quickly back when Chi hissed. Fear crawled up the old man's back as the neck snaked out and bared gleaming fangs.

"Hold, evil one. The enemy is dead and he wishes

to help you."

Raven admonished his angry mount, but Chi did not spare anyone from his baleful gaze and drooling fangs. The hair-raising moan increased if anyone passed to closely.

"Yes, yes only to help. I have medicines..."

"Water, if you may spare it and rags. I must cleanse the wounds and mix the powders to close them."

"Yes, this I may do. A moment..."

The old man hurried away to return with two large buckets of precious water. He sat them down well away from the thing that could not be a horse. They were Thanatu, had saved many lives today. Surely the lord would reward them and any kindness to them would reflect well upon him. The Thanatu acknowledged his return with grim smile and carried the buckets away. The creature buried his nose in one drinking noisily. The Aja washed the worst of the torn flesh, not horse quivering and snorting during the process.

"The other animals are stabled master. Frightened, but only minor cuts and bruising from the fallen stones."

"That is good to know. Ullric would try to kill it again if he lost his horse. There are few strong enough to bare his weight and nowhere on the blasted plain to find another."

"Indeed master. He is a very levelheaded beast, I must say. He calmed right down when I approached him. I was worried because he is so big."

"He is very docile. That is a good thing for his rider is of different ilk."

"Yes he is very fierce. I have never seen any man fight like him. And you throw yourself again and again against impossible odds. My bowels watered when I heard that scream. I could not raise a hand to help my lord. It is my shame."

"Nonsense. You are obviously not trained to fight. What could you have done but find your death in this forsaken place? You serve your lord as you were trained to do. No more is expected."

"As you say. Is this the end of the horrors that have plagued my lord?"

"I cannot speak of this to you old man. I think it is time you returned to the stables."

Startled by the sudden change in demeanor, the man hurried away. He certainly did not wish ill will to replace the warrior's previous regard.

It was some time before Ullric returned, Jin and Jivita on his heels and two of their servants loaded down with packs and boxes. They raced to their lord and bowed before him. The silent conversation went on for some time then the wives departed to the barracks.

Jaap pushed himself up once more brushing aside his insistent servants. He sent messages of assurance to his wives and mother, sequestered and heavily guarded in the manor. Across the yard the blonde one carefully laid a pack on the ground then backed carefully away from the slavering beast. The Aja sat down in the dust and opened the bag. He spent some time weighing and stirring various powders in small bowls. Eventually he turned to the animal and filled the wounds with the pastes all the while crooning in the Aja tongue. Jaap had no idea if it was a spell for healing or to keep the creature from killing them all. The Aja completed his task and walked across the yard to stand at the foot of the steps.

"I ask a favor lord of Guerdon. My mount needs meat, fresh kill to regain his strength. I would need a horse to bring it back from the market place."

"You need not burden yourself with this task, warrior."

So saying Jaap hailed two of his soldiers and instructed them to bring a bullock from the animal pens. The men hurried away through another smaller gate between the blacksmith and cook shed. It wasn't long before they returned dragging an agitated ox into the yard. It bawled at the smell of rotting carrion and gore tossing its head violently. Chi's head came up and the snap of fangs echoed in the yard.

"Take it to the stables away from the other animals. It would not do for anyone to witness Chi feeding."

Jaap nodded and the men dragged the ox off to the

barn. In a few minutes they were back, the agitated handler scurrying behind them. Raven walked along side as Chi made the slow painful journey to the barn. The Thanatu left him at the door and returned to the lord's side. It was not long before a bawl of terror was heard. It continued until fear once again gripped every man, then ceased. Much later, the men in the barracks would sleep uneasily, the sounds of bones snapping adding to their list of frightening dreams.

"How, where should we dispose of this creature Aja? We burned the thing it birthed, but the stench of this..."

"Drag it onto the waste from your nearest gate. If you can clear the streets no one may see it go. That is, if you have horses enough for the dragging. Leave it as a warning to others who think to take what this day you have fought to hold. If you burn it many of your people will be ill from the smoke."

"Even now my men are stricken beneath its stench."

"Chi's venom is dangerous as well, the combination could be lethal."

The order was given and the young man invited Aja and his companion to enter his home.

"I have but poor accommodations to offer Aja, but your company may partake of all I have."

"I for one could use a tankard of ale. Killing beast is thirsty work."

Ullric smacked his lips in anticipation of a good meal and perhaps willing company. The lord gave orders and servants took the blonde giant in hand. He allowed them to lead him away.

"And you Aja?"

"I would speak with you of the events of the day."

"As you wish. Come this way. Jola, food, water and wine in my sanctuary."

The man hurried away and Jaap lead Raven through the many hallways and up the stairs. The room took up most of the second floor with an open balcony above a rock garden. Statues of the deities the plain dwellers worshiped stood on engraved stone amid colored sand presenting an intricate flower like pattern. Scrolls of many materials were shelved in slots on one entire wall of the room. At the back windows a large table sat with scrolls, carved paint boxes and drawing sticks scattered across its surface. A stone chair faced it, padded with black-spiced pillows. There were only two other chairs in the room. One directly opposite the desk and one before a great stone fireplace, precious wood kindling stacked next to it. Raven noticed scroll work only around doorways, scripted in beaten gold. The remaining walls were stark white In contrast to the murals and filigree that marked Jirair's home.

Raven set before the desk and Jaap took the other. He quickly cleared the scattered items, slightly embarrassed at the mess. Servants came and washed them of the worse. Jaap promised Raven a real bath after their talk. They sat in silence until the servants completed serving then consumed two goblets of hot wine. It rushed through Raven's system and he switched to water after a few mouthfuls of bread and meat. More at ease than he expected Jaap served Aja marveling at the sheer size of him. And to think the blonde one was even bigger. The power behind his blows was a shocking thing to see. No wonder they plied the mercenary trade, one man holding such warriors could conquer a world. He shook himself free of such thoughts, after all, he was Guerdon and destiny demanded he rule and die here.

Raven was very aware of the lord's attention. Some of the thoughts showed clearly on his youthful face. Like most people in the city, he was tall and slim, though not weak. He was muscled from long hours of practice with sword and wrestling. Lines of care marked him now, dimming the blue, almost gray eyes. His silk garments were torn and dirty, damp with sweat and blood. Wide gold bracelets encircled his slim wrists. Although, he did not appear to be arrogant as many landholders were, the Thanatu was wary.

He would not become the kept pet of any man who ruled over others, no matter how benevolent. His thoughts turned unwillingly to Jerred and he hoped the young one fared well. It would please him to find Mabe mate to the young man if he ever returned to the North Country. But to the business at hand. He sat back in the chair, relaxed and a little sleepy.

"Jaap Guerdon the creature we killed this day was a beast I did not believe existed. The women of Thanatu tell of many such things and I have seen etchings. If Chi was not with us today we would not have prevailed. His venom prevented it from healing and finally killed it. Know who ever conjured such a beast is here within the city and close to you."

"Close to me? You cannot mean in my household? My servants are loyal and the guards are the most elite of the city troop."

"I only know this is true. The guards are not under suspicion I think. Whoever it is must be close enough to pull nightmares from your mind to do this thing."

"You cannot be saying I dream of such abomination and make it live."

"Jaap hear me. To end this you must trust, or live ever under the spell of this evil until all are dead. One terror in the night, even as a child, would remain in your mind for this sorcerer to choose."

The lord laughed, he fell back in his chair and laughed harder. Raven sat patiently as the laughter continued until Jaap fell to weeping, finally collapsing onto the desktop. It was some time before the tears ended.   Servants hovered in the doorway, fear and concern on their faces. Finally he raised his head, snaring one of the lap clothes to wipe his face. He gripped the goblet with both hands and Raven poured wine into it. Jaap dragged it to his lips with shaking hands, choking before he was able to swallow the lukewarm brew. When he drained the cup, he sat a moment more in silence.

"What must I do Aja? How may I atone for this disaster?"

"You atone for nothing lord. You carry no guilt in this. Someone covets all you have. What you must do is be prepared to sacrifice the one who is the creator of your pain, regardless the identity of the evil one."

"You are saying that I must kill someone I trust, maybe love to end my torment?

"Know that once you set the cure in motion, even I cannot call it back. Chi is kin to things unknown and some say demonic and I cannot stop him if the prey exists here. Once set loose, retribution will not be stopped. Any between him and the sorcerer will fall as well."

Jaap sat back and stared at the warrior before him. That the creature he rode was not as it seemed was obvious with its gleaming fangs and forked tongue. Could he watch someone he loved die based on a strangers notions? What to do? He thought of Jatara and her babe taken then replaced with the thing he had cared for. How long had she been dead? What horrors had she suffered? Who could do such a thing to an innocent loving woman and her babe? His heart ached with the memory of three other precious babes lost in a year's time. All of them born healthy, only to die within days. It was abomination to harm a child. By the gods what must he do? He buried his head in his hands as tears threatened once more.

Raven waited patiently. He was bruised and exhausted, craving a flat surface to sleep. Chi was sore and enraged at being set upon. His desire for vengeance permeated Raven's mind, a relentless haranguing beating in time with his pulse.

"What must I do Aja? I wish my family safe as any man. From what you say the only thing saving us the first time was the thing giving birth prematurely. But how can I condemn one close to me to death on a strangers words?"

Raven did not respond to the query. He sat back in the chair to stare at the man faced with a monumental decision. The answer was within. Raven could not help.

There was a sudden disturbance at the entrance to the room and Jola rushed in bowing to his lord. With a quick suspicious glance at the Aja, the agitated servant signed some urgent message and waited for his lord's response.

"The captain and his wives seek audience with me Aja. Jola says they have gathered up your giant friend and insist on the sight of you. Bring them Jola, I am curious."

Jirair stalked into his lords' presence, his head was thickly bandaged, but he moved with his natural grace. He was stripped to black armor and weapons strapped down tightly for battle. His wives clothes were wrinkled and stained with blood and filth from treating the wounded. They went to their knees before the lord and Jirair bowed low. Ullric gave everyone a glare of distaste over bowing and scraping to a mere man born to what he did not earn with sword or axe.

"My lord. Rumors have spread within the city about the creature attacking the manor. Many fear to remain and exhort all to flee. The guard has quelled one riot. I have closed the taverns and commanded everyone to their homes. Five men are dead and at least twenty seriously wounded or gravely ill. Jivin says it must be removed quickly or more men will die."

"I ordered it dragged away before I came in Jirair. Speak to Joost, the east gate is not very wide but fewer people live there to see this thing. Use as many horses as necessary. If I must pay a few more coins to the water dealers, it is of no consequence. See that a messenger is sent to them that I will pay extra for an increase in delivery for the next moon."

"It will be as you say my lord. I would send Jin home to the children with your permission."

"Of course, do so immediately. Have Joost send two of my own to attend her safely."

"Jivin will remain here until the carcass is removed and the men are recovering on their own."

"Jarair, once again your devotion is displayed for all men to see. My heart is joyful and secure knowing you protect my city."

Jaap removed a wide gold band from his arm and Jirair stepped back in shock.

"My lord I cannot..."

"I command you Jarair. This very day my life was saved by one you brought to my attention. Today the curse will be lifted from my house and peace will reign in Guerdon once more, because of you captain. No one serves me so well as your household. Take this useless bauble and wear it beneath your sleeve. Oh yes, I know that you are envied because my father favored your marriages into noble houses. But know this, any that raise hand against you from this day will face my wrath. Go now attend my will. Jin go to your house with my thanks for your service this day."

He opened his arms wide and Jin and Javin stepped forward for his kiss to their foreheads. Bowing low they retreated to Raven's side and kissed his cheek relieved that he was only bruised. He returned their kisses and they left with Jola guiding them from the room. Jirair bowed to his lord and left to carry out his assignments. He did not acknowledge Raven because it would seem an insult to his lord. Ullric arose from the seat he had taken by the fireplace his eyes on the Thanatu.

"So what happens now? Do you know who we must find to end this?"

"I do not know who as yet, only that they must reside within this place."

"It is a hard thing to think one of my own would seek to destroy me."

The blonde giant growled.

"I tell you man, if there is rot in your dwelling wait not for it to spread or everything will be lost to you. I know."

Ullric's face clouded.

"Jaap has yet to decide what will be done. It is his city and if he desires it we will leave things as they are and go on our way."

"No Aja. The signs are too obvious for me to ignore. I hear the truth in your words. If I do nothing my family is in grave danger. More babes will die. I would know. I would know if it tears out my heart."

"Be prepared lord of this cursed place. If the Thanatu ferrets out your poison it will cost you dearly, but better the cleansing than more death and fear."

Ullric poured the remaining wine from the pitcher to Raven's cup and drank it down.

"So what do we do Aja?"

"If you are sure Jaap."

The lord took a deep breath and let it out slowly. He rubbed his bloodshot eyes and sighed.

"I wished my life free of this taint and my city secure. In this I am yours to command."

"I will need a room bare of furnishing. All of your household without exception must come before me. When the root of evil appears Chi will strike. Think not to raise hand against me for the life I take Jaap. There will be no question of guilt. The stench of this creature will linger on its creator."

"I swear on my father's heart that I will honor my decision Aja. I would sleep in peace and watch my children grow if the gods will grant me more."

"It is done."

With that remark Raven and Jaap rose from the chairs.

"Be ready Ullric. I would have you at my side. If we are attacked between Chi and you any creature should be vanquished."

"So be it Thanatu. I do not understand how Chi will do this. Do you plan for the accused to face you in the barn?"

The remark forced a grim chuckle from Raven.

"No, you will see soon enough. Jaap if you would prepare the room? The strongest of your guard must stand ready at the door. When each person enters they must bar it from the outside. Ullric will knock three times if it is safe to open and release them."

"It will be done."

Jaap hurried away, his stomach cramping at the horrible possibilities awaiting his house.

"Ullric, listen well. You know that Chi and I have a bond of great strength. Today I will take myself to the deepest part of him and remain. Chi will be at your side to find the sorcerer."

All the fine hair on Ullric body waved as a cold shiver raced up his back and left him with fear flesh. Unconsciously, he rubbed his arms to remove the chill.

"Do not speak to him. Do not touch my body. He is as unpredictable as you are in battle rage. Follow his commands without hesitation. If need be help him kill the sorcerer or the one he works through. Can you do this?"

"No man can name me coward, Thanatu. Do what you must, but know that your body or not, I will not let that cursed beast kill me without a fight."

"Chi will not kill you."

"And you are so sure of this, why?

"I asked him not to."

"Ha! I have seen how quick he is to obey you."

Ullric snorted and followed Raven from the room.

Jaap met them in the hallway the ever-present Jola on his heels.

"It has been done as you wish Aja."

"I will need a candle mark to prepare Jaap. Then bring me all the members of you household, one by one, without exception. Understand no one is exempt. Start with those closest to you and tell them nothing."

Jaap stared at Raven a moment longer.

"A candle mark. As you say. Come...come this way."

So not yet done. More time...more time to worry. More time for fear. Jaap did not know if he could survive more of this without losing his mind. My wives and mother first. That can only mean the Aja suspects them. It cannot be. I cannot think of what that would mean.

The room was on the ground floor level but at the rear of the house down a long hallway. There were many rooms along each side. Jaap explained they were stores for the household and furniture his ancestors used. Two of the household guards were standing in front of a door. One held an iron bar nearly six feet long in his hand. The ornate handles of the door were just curved enough the bar would slide between them. It should be sufficient to prevent anyone from leaving. The hallway was narrow and Raven could foresee another problem.

"This will take some time. You will need to bring them one at a time and remain until they are done. Be sure to deliver them to separate quarters when the meeting is concluded so they do not speak to the others."

"I will see to it Aja. You men, hear me well. This is the Aja obey him without questions. Whatever you hear do not open these doors until he or the blonde one speaks. To do so may unleash another such as we fought today."

The men shifted nervously. They were still shaken by the morning's events and would have preferred latrine duty than to guard this door.

"As you command, my lord."

They spoke as one, though sweat had already began to appear above their lips. Raven entered the room without another word, Ullric at his back. The barbarian pulled the door shut and laughed when he heard the bar scrap across the handles of the door.

"It will take me some time to complete this Ullric. You should sit for now and stand before the door when the household members enter."

"It will be as you say Thanatu. Just remind that evil nag not to make any sudden moves."

"Chi will not harm you big fool. There is much greater danger for all of us than Chi."

"I took an axe to one great danger today boy, another will not vex me."

Raven gave up the argument. Ullric was as stubborn as an ox and more worried about Chi than any creature four stories tall. He supposed the man had some good explanation for the appearance of the creature they fought today, but now was not the time for it. He went to his knees to begin his breathing exercises.

Soon he was aware of nothing.

It was just short of the hour when Raven inhaled deeply and raised his head. Ullric stood cautiously and backed against the door. The eyes were not the Thanatu's, oh no. They were dark as night with no whites around them. The barbarian licked his lips and tried to calm his sudden racing pulse. The face smiled, but it was all teeth and menace.

"Cold--man. Small times speak mine."

The voice was Raven's but hesitant, like the whispers of the dead in the night. Fear flesh covered Ullric from scalp to toes. It stunned him to realize that he believed he was actually listening to the creature in the barn. Somehow he knew, though how he could not say, that Raven was truly gone.

"Fear…good cold man. Fear me…good."

Ullric wanted to curse it, kill it. His terror, and he had to finally acknowledge it with that in the room, choked him. Raven said not to speak and he must not. But oh, to shout his denial and kill it.

"Dark light, one." The hissing whisper seemed to

be inside his head so fear sweat beaded across Ullric's back.

Not Raven's head cocked to one side as if expecting an answer. Do I understand? Ullric believed he did and nodded.

"Pain pain pain Chi not kill--brave mine."

Ullric nodded again. Raven had the scars to prove what a terrible trial he endured to have this, whatever Chi was at his side."

"Men fear. You dare fear. Why this?"

Ullric did not know what to do. Raven said not to speak but this was a direct question. If he did not answer would Chi take offense? Silence for a long moment, then...

"Fear me you. Stay why?"

"I...I have nothing to go back to. Jerred's place confines me. If I do not fall on my sword I must learn to live in this world. Raven said I would not trouble him and could learn to trade my axe for gold."

"Why this?"

The cold voice was deeper and Ullric stirred uneasily. What could he say?

"The boy is my equal in battle. He is fearless and I have never seen the like of you before."

He blinked and not Raven was before him swaying slightly. The level of danger increased tenfold. He could not bear to look into the eyes and turned away, the truth was forced from his lips.

My pe--my people do--did--not sit alone at the fire by choice."

"Thanatu take, Thanatu keep, Thanatu mine not."

"But you are with him. What do you mean not Thanatu?"

"Pain mine. Thanatu clan keeps not. Pain mine... clan not."

Ullric mulled that over for a moment. It was hard to think with Raven's body so near and that feral grin on its face.

"You mean he is Thanatu."

The body shifted.

"But he could not stay with them. He is not like them."

"Pain, pain, pain live. Mine Thanatu. Mine not Thanatu."

"Cursed beast, what are you saying? Pain before he was Thanatu, pain after. Raven could not stay because even with you the pain did not stop. What pain, what do you mean?"

There was another long silence while the unwavering gaze held him trapped in darkness.

"Fire pain--one."

The questions were threatening to choke him. He wanted to understand. Maybe in order to live with this thing in some peace he had to ask.

"Raven's like me, no one the same. He would not sit alone at the fire."

"Mine, all time mine. Cursed to join light--"

Frustration marked not Raven's face, heavy shoulders rolled back and muscle seemed to flow like snakes beneath the shirt. The sudden movement startled Ullric, but he stood his ground.

"So you stay with Raven forever?"

"Mine fall, go I. Mine not, stay."

The grin got wider, unnaturally so. For a moment Ullric thought his response was wrong. Had not Raven's teeth grown sharper?

"Cold man sit, mine sit. Pain not—all."

Oh, Ullric thought he understood.

"He has stood between me and Tor's halls many times since I met him. I will share the fire as long as he wishes it."

"Mine cold man...re...mem...ber mine, all time. Mine pain...pain you."

The low staccato growl that always raised Ullric's hair arrested the protest he thought to make.

"Prey comes."

In a blink not Raven knelt once more on the floor and the guards pulled the door wide.

"Jaap I really do not understand why I must meet these..."

The woman voice trailed away as she beheld the

kneeling man.

"What is the meaning of this? Jaap, what are you doing?"

The woman turned back to the heavy doors in surprise, her white, gold trimmed skirt lifting to expose golden sandals on her feet.

"Open this door!"

"Jaap not. You stay. Answer."

"Stay, answer? Open the door this instant!"

Jeran was first wife of the previous lord and mother to Jaap. Although she despaired of his judgment many times, she was always treated with utmost respect. Angry she turned back to the kneeling man glancing warily at the barbarian in the corner. Her hands shook, but did not disturb the gold bracelets, which covered her arms from wrists to elbows. The perfumed oil in her dark graying hair permeated the room. Jeweled baubles glittered in the curls and around her neck.

"Who are you?" She demanded of not Raven.

"Answer. Smell you. Blood you," he whispered.

"Smell, smell?", Jeran squeaked, "What madness is this?"

Blood rushed to her cheeks in embarrassment. She had never been so--so insulted in her life.

"You will not speak to me in such a manner. Jaap, open this door!"

She beat at the door with her fist, fear finally

obliterating her anger. All the air left her lungs in a rush as adrenaline stole the strength form her limbs.

She turned back to her jailers as a hair raising growl rose up from the man thing on the floor."

"What, what is it you want?"

Then he looked up and she saw the black pits where his eyes should be and a mouth wide with sharp white—

In the corridor Jaap fell to his knees and the guards turned to face the door with swords drawn. The scream went on and on.

Ullric held his axe before him a hair's breadth from cutting down the terrorized woman. Chi stood over her shrieking form until she lay whimpering at his feet.

"Why babes, wives--son die?"

Ullric shuddered under the influence of Chi's wheedling hiss.

"I advised. I fought for it all. His father was weak and he is no better. The metal we need to survive is now but a trickle. He pays the rabble to work instead of keeping them in chains. Outsiders come take our gold to make the tunnels safe. He takes wives from the lesser houses and the other cities, for love he says. The alliances of a thousand years are tossed aside."

"Name them."

He shook her.

"Name them."

Jeran refused to look directly at Chi.

She smiled through the tears and mucus on her face.

"I will tell you nothing. I--no, no by the gods no!"

She screamed again has Chi lifted her closer to his grinning mouth. She kicked and wailed, the names of her co-conspirators spilling in an incoherent babble.

"Spell--spell weaver."

"I do not know. By the gods I do not know."

"False wretch!"

The depthless eyes stared into hers. She moaned, tore at her hair and shrieked. Her neck snapped so loudly Ullric leaped to Chi's side before he realized what the sound really meant.

"Spell weaver here not. We go."

Ullric pounded on the door calling Jaap until he heard the bar slide away.

Chi knocked the guards aside and raced down the hall.

The NorBlad followed the swiftly moving form to the third level. Chi put his shoulder to a door and crashed through. Shrill laughter greeted his entrance. The NorBlad gagged on the foul smoke pouring from the room.

"To late, barbarians. Everyone will die."

Jola made no move to avoid the warrior's attack. He knew they would be overcome very quickly. He was not prepared for the metal door to bang shut leaving the dark haired one surrounded by the noxious black fumes filling the air. A deaths head rictus stretched the mouth unnaturally wide exposing stilettos of gleaming white. The servant was stunned and backed away from the apparition. Chi growled.

"Spell weaver, life giver no more," not Raven hissed.

"No this is not possible. What are you?"

"What seek you? For you I."

The man was confused by the last response and frowned. He did not realize he was moving around the stone pedestal where the glass tube emitting the dark spell rested. The Aja crushed the tube under his fist and grinned wider at the traitorous servant. His fangs glittered like sun on snow within the clouds of smoke.

Jola only knew he was on the floor when the death grip on his throat eased up enough to let in just a bit of the poisoned air. The Aja swayed, hissing interspersed with guttural words. The spell reversed before his eyes. Dark clouds rolled back to spin and spin until he shut his eyes against the sickening motion. The barbarian's gibbering rose to a piercing wail before his hard thick thumb pressed into Jola's cheek and forced his mouth open. Then he noticed the funnel spinning tighter and tighter, rushing toward him. Jola struggled ineffectively against the strength in the big hands even after the vapor covered his face and disappeared.

Chi held the man close, forcing the nose and mouth shut. Blisters appeared on the surface of his skin and it reddened. The servant kicked wildly, snapping his own bones against the pain as his body swelled and cracked. His blood and internal organs slowly dissolved. When the body ceased to jerk and tremble not Raven left it. He never made it to the door.

Ullric thought he heard someone call his name. It was dark. Something foul twisted and lurched in his belly. He gritted his teeth against the cramps and cursed Tor for allowing him to die with a bellyache. Suddenly his body expelled the invader leaving the barbarian unconscious against the wall. Again and again his name was heard until the irritation roused him from the stupor the black smoke caused. The door! Lurching to his feet he blindly shook off the hands that attempted to assist him. He put his shoulder to the metal but it did not yield. Angered, Ullric swung his axe piercing the thin sheet of metal until he finally sheared the joints from the wall. The door rocked but did not fall so it was hurled aside with a snarl.

The Thanatu's body lay face down. Ullric staggered forward, snatched the heavy body from the floor and passed out.

Water sellers tripled their deliveries to

accommodate the enormous amounts used by Jaap's ravaged household. He took the bodies of his mother and servant beyond the city boundary and left them to rot. He spoke a curse to follow where the spore from the demon servant originated. Then turned his men back to Guerdon where acolytes of the gods traveled though out the city waving braziers of incense to bless and reassure the people. The men who risked their lives for his city were very sick. It was feared Aja would die. Jaap offered sacrifice to the gods and asked his people to pray for Aja's recovery. It was all they could do.

Raven's eyes snapped open. Hands were laid upon him as he jerked upright to vomit in excruciating spasms until exhaustion dragged him down once more.

In a coma for days, his now fitful consciousness was plagued with fevered delirium and violent spasms. He called out in several languages, cursed and wept. He tried to fight, but the enemy tied him and Chi did not come.

Ullric held the sweat slicked arms as Raven heaved and screamed beneath him. Several of the guard assisted as Jin and Jivin tried to force-feed him another herbal mixture. Raven slipped into a coma once again.

"You must rest Ullric. It will take time to regain your strength." Jin signed, pressing her slim hands against the broad chest drenched in sweat and still fevered from his own brush with death.

"I will rest after we take him to the stables."

"Stables? Why would you want to do this?"

"He is dying Jin. I think your potions have little effect. Perhaps the beast's venom will spare him or end his suffering."

Jin wanted to protest, but Jivin's desperate efforts had proved of little use against the foul vapor. She stepped aside and Jivin rose from the bedside. His slim figure trembled with fatigue. His clothes were damp and wrinkled.

Jivin signed.

"He is correct my love. I can do no more."

The healer's eyes filled with tears. He could not save the Aja, friend of his husband and savior of their lord.

"Forgive me Ullric. I…"

The barbarian stroked his heavy hand across the damp curls on the healer's head. Jin held Jivin close as he wept, shamed by his failure.

"You are not to at fault healer. The twice-cursed servant is to blame. Help me. If I drop his heavy carcass Chi will take my life."

Guards, stripped down to tunic and breeches hurried to the barbarian's side to help him lift the inert body onto his shoulders. Ullric staggered still weakened from his own ordeal. The men took Raven's weight until the giant regained his balance and shuffled slowly out of the room. They held close to his back, down the hall and the narrow stairways to the first floor. The main floor of the manor was dark, its master in seclusion with his remaining wives. The servants slept, free at last from washing walls and floors with herbal concoctions to eliminate the stench of dark magic. The guard pulled the doors wide, startling the four men on watch from the porch and inner yard.

"Hold, all is well. We take the Aja to his magical beast. Perhaps it will cure him."

The men stood aside, one shaking his head in doubt that anything could save the assassin after so many died from tainted blood and wounds.

Javas ran ahead to open the stable doors then continued in his fellow's footsteps, tracking the barbarian to the center of the gated stalls.

"No further, the beast will take exception."

They watched as the big man called out, speaking as if the beast could understand.

"He is dying. Will you save him or take your freedom."

Ullric dropped Raven's body before the stall leaping aside quickly as fangs snapped shut inches from his chest.

"Let him die Chi and leave this place." Ullric

taunted moving along the far wall. The barbarian and guards slipped quickly from the stable.

Just as Ullric's patience was hard pressed to wait a moment longer, Raven's hoarse cries of pain could be heard through the door. So the beast did strike. Maybe his venom would not kill the Thanatu as it cleansed the other poisons from his body. Morning would be soon enough to know. He was tired and still sick to his stomach. Having done what he could the barbarian made his way to bed, the guards occasionally righting his drifting shuffle into the manor.

Raven shivered and howled throughout the night. The sun was well into its morning climb when the last of the combined poisons were purged. He passed into a coma like sleep assured his connection to Chi remained.

Days later the warriors were returned to Jirair's home. The lord's manor was inundated with petitioners, ambassadors, servants and extended members of his wives families. The atmosphere was almost hysterically jubilant. It was no place for irritable, sick to the stomach warriors to recover.

Jaap was hollow eyed with shock at his mother's betrayal, but turned his grief to revenge stoked punishment for the city's betrayers. The conspirators from the old families were executed in the public squares, angry citizens clamoring for their deaths for the heinous crime of killing children. Their families were stripped of wealth and condemned to the mines without pay to serve Guerdon for life. The children were fostered into homes of those loyal to Jaap. He began an obsessive hunt for protective spells to prevent any further encroachment on members of his household and his city.

Raven reclined in pillowed splendor on the front porch. He knew that a few more weeks must pass before they were ready to move on. Jirair's men patrolled the streets insuring the continued privacy of his quests. Laughter erupted somewhere in the depths of the house. Raven relaxed into his dark companion's mind and dozed.

They would depart with gold and supplies to keep them for a great length of days. He would miss Jirair and his family. These affectionate people were the closest he would ever come to a clan of his own. For all the pain Ullric suffered, Raven envied him the past.

The End

About the Author

Born in New Orleans, La. and lived in Alexandria until she was twelve, Patricia I. Williams fell in love with Southern California on arrival. She would not want to live anywhere else, at least for this lifetime. She loves knowing the ocean is just beyond the hill and that Disneyland is the happiest place on earth. She enjoys traveling through the Southwest. The history and legends fuel a lot of imaginative Wild West adventures. She loves Science Fiction, film and books. Believes horses, dogs and cats are ideal companions.

Her faith in Jehovah keeps her grounded. She believes one lifetime is not long enough to learn everything. She is wary of all information because it most often is dependent on the good intentions of the provider. These days she finds pleasure is seeing her grandchildren's curiosity about the world around them.